SPECIAL MESSAGE TO READERS

THE ULVERSCROFT FOUNDATION
(registered UK charity number 264873)
was established in 1972 to provide funds for research, diagnosis and treatment of eye diseases. Examples of major projects funded by the Ulverscroft Foundation are:-

- The Children's Eye Unit at Moorfields E[illegible] Hospital, London
- The Ulverscroft Children's Eye Unit at Gre[illegible] Ormond Street Hospital for Sick Children
- Funding research into eye diseases a[illegible] treatment at the Department of Ophthalmolo[illegible] University of Leicester
- The Ulverscroft Vision Research Grou[illegible] Institute of Child Health
- Twin operating theatres at the West[illegible] Ophthalmic Hospital, London
- The Chair of Ophthalmology at the R[illegible] Australian College of Ophthalmologists

You can help further the work of the Foundati[illegible] by making a donation or leaving a legacy. Every contribution is gratefully received. If yo[illegible] would like to help support the Foundation o[illegible] require further information, please contact:

THE ULVERSCROFT FOUNDATION
The Green, Bradgate Road, Anstey
Leicester LE7 7FU, England
Tel: (0116) 236 4325
website: www.foundation.ulverscroft.com

CODE OF SILENCE

When Sterling Seabright is found strangled in the woods outside the small farming community of Abundance, Wisconsin, even her closest friends are shocked to learn of her secret life. When a second body is found murdered in a cabin by the lake, it's up to Deputies Robely Danner and Frack Tilsley to discover the link. Sterling's classmates hold various pieces of the puzzle, and although they may be talking among themselves, Robely and Frack are unable to break their code of silence . . .

Books by Arlette Lees
in the Linford Mystery Library:

ANGEL DOLL

ARLETTE LEES

CODE OF SILENCE

Complete and Unabridged

LINFORD
Leicester

First published in Great Britain

First Linford Edition
published 2014

A catalogue record for this book is available from the British Library.

ISBN 978–1–4448–2231–1

Published by
F. A. Thorpe (Publishing)
Anstey, Leicestershire

Set by Words & Graphics Ltd.
Anstey, Leicestershire
Printed and bound in Great Britain by
T. J. International Ltd., Padstow, Cornwall

This book is printed on acid-free paper

1

When the lights of town vanish from the rear view mirror and he turns onto the two-lane highway, headed away from their usual destination, the picture-pretty girl in the passenger seat has the feeling something isn't quite right. He's been awfully quiet since she got in the car, no longer the carefree, outgoing guy he was a few short months ago. With every mile she feels the gulf widen between them. The woods are deep and dark on both sides of the road, the moon cut into puzzle pieces by the twisted branches of trees.

In the beginning they were carefree lovers, meeting in secret; every sense tuned to a fever pitch. Music was more moving than before, colors brighter, flowers more fragrant. It was like nothing could come between them. That's the way love is supposed to be, isn't it? Then came a shift, a subtle cooling, like when the summer goes and your tan fades and the last of the sun slips through a crack in the season.

'Is something wrong?' A stupid question, but she asks it anyway.

'What could possibly be wrong?' he says, with a tight smile that isn't much of a smile at all. The earth wobbles slightly on its axis and she feels an uncomfortable twist in the pit of her stomach. It's as if she's climbed into the car with a stranger.

'You're going the wrong way. We're going to the cabin, remember?'

'We can't,' he says. 'The old bat in 5 told my dad that someone's been using the place.'

'But, she doesn't know it's us . . . does she?'

'I don't know, but we're pushing our luck. Dad's no idiot.'

She sits quietly, watching the dark trees blur by. 'That leaves the motel in Weyauwega. No one will recognize us there.'

'Not tonight.'

'Then where are we going?'

His head whips toward her. 'Would you

shut up? Can't you see how annoying you are?' The muscles in his jaw flex and a pulse throbs in his temple. 'Just stop talking,' he says, more quietly. 'I'm driving to settle my nerves.'

She's stunned into silence, but only for a moment.

'If you didn't want to see me you should have cancelled,' she says. 'I could be studying for class instead of wasting my time.'

'I am cancelling. After tonight I won't be seeing you anymore.'

'You don't mean you're dumping me?' Her big, blue eyes study his face in the semi-darkness of the car.

He snorts a laugh. 'You had no problem dumping Carl.'

'How can you say that? I left him for you.'

'I guess what goes around comes around. Besides, you knew this relationship had a limited shelf life. If you pretended it was anything more than a fling you're delusional.'

She unconsciously touches her midsection.

The gesture doesn't go unnoticed. 'You can't turn your back on me now.'

'Oh, I heard the rumor.'

She gasps. 'That's impossible!'

'Is it? If you think so, you have something to learn about small towns.'

'You came on to me, remember? You're in this as deep as I am.'

'Not quite.'

'You think I'm going to let you walk away like nothing happened?'

'Oh, something happened all right.' He takes in her soft tangle of golden hair, those long toned legs and slender torso. 'What healthy male wouldn't want some of that?'

'You took advantage of me,' she says. 'You're a fraud.'

'What, you're going to play the martyr now? Don't try to tell me this was your first rodeo. From what I've heard, you're quite the little cowgirl.'

'You made promises. You lied to me.'

He gives her an icy glance. 'Guys lie to get girls in the sack and girls pretend to believe them. Besides, you got what I got in equal measure and came back for more. I never said I loved you. Not once. I couldn't resist you. There's a big difference.'

There's a break in the trees and moonlight flashes across the hood of the car. His teeth clench, the skin pulled tight across his cheekbones. Gloves peek from his jacket pocket, but in the dim light from the dash they don't look at all like his pigskin driving gloves. The forest thickens and the moon goes into hiding.

'There's no sense driving in this direction if we're not going anyplace. You're just wasting gas,' she says. 'I want to go back.'

'There is no going back.' The finality in his tone frightens her. He steps on the gas and launches the car deeper into the night

'If you don't take me back to town I'm telling my father when I get home and I'm going to see Sheriff Brooker in the morning. I don't allow people to treat me like this.' When the car hits 60 it begins to vibrate. 'Slow down. You're scaring me.'

He pushes the vehicle further over the speed limit, his eyes riveted on the road ahead.

She suddenly rips the gloves from his pocket and feels the surgical rubber between her fingers. With a shrill cry she explodes and lands a barrage of adrenaline-fueled blows to his head. He cringes from the surprising power of her fists. She jerks the steering wheel and sets the car zigzagging recklessly across the center line. An oncoming driver leans on the horn and swerves to avoid a head-on collision. He slams her back against the seat with a stiff forearm, steps on the brake and struggles to regain control of the car.

'Stop the car! Stop the goddamn car!' she says, yanking the door handle.

The door flies open, the wind nearly tearing it from its hinges. They skid to a stop on the gravel shoulder and teeter on the edge of the ditch. By the time he clears the driver's seat the girl is running along the road with strong athletic strides, her shrieks and sobs swallowed by the wind that sweeps the isolated woods.

There's no time to think. He wrestles the gloves onto his hands and pounds down the highway after her.

* * *

Carl Hammond lies awake in the garden cottage behind the main house. It has a bed, a small bath, a couple wicker chairs and a space heater, every amenity a high school senior could hope for. It's past midnight, wind thrashing the treetops and a shower of leaves spinning across the roof. His cell phone rings and he rolls over with a sleepy moan.

'Sterling?' he says.

'No, it's me, Madison.'

'Oh.'

'Don't sound so enthusiastic.'

'Do you know what time it is?'

'I had to wait until my parents were asleep,' she says.

'Why? What's going on?' He sits up and swings his legs over the side of the bed, his face reflected in the window across from him. His features are chiseled and classic, his blond hair stylishly short on the sides and long on top like a California surfer.

'Have you heard from Sterling?' she asks. He yawns and flips his hair off his forehead.

'No. You?'

'Nothing. It's freaking me out.'

'What do you expect?' he says. 'You acted like a nut case the other night.'

'She had it coming. You know she did.'

'Did it ever occur to you that you might be wrong about her? I don't see Eddie as being her type at all.'

'Think about it. She kicked you to the curb at the same time Eddie left me.'

'Alright, so we're rid of her. I don't know what else to tell you.'

'I'm afraid it's more complicated than that. On Wednesday she asked if it would be okay to tell her parents she was staying with me for a few days. I only said yes because I thought we might be friends again like we used to be. Now she's taken off and refuses to answer her cell phone.'

'After Thursday night, what do you expect? You got physical. You stepped over the line.'

'She gave as good as she got.' Madison touches the scratches on her face. 'She hasn't been in class and if her parents come looking for her I don't know what to tell them. Do you have any idea where she's gone?'

'In case you've forgotten, she's my ex-girlfriend. She doesn't provide me with her daily itinerary.' He knows more than he's telling, but this isn't the time to share it. Wind rattles the cottage window and rose vines scrape the shingle siding. 'Let's sit on it a day or two and see what happens. If her parents show up, tell the truth.'

Once Madison is off the line, Carl lies back with his arms behind his head and stares at the ceiling. When Sterling broke up with him he didn't hear from her again . . . until last week. Now their lives are entangled in a way he never anticipated

'I'm pregnant,' she said, getting right to the point. There was a moment's disorientation before he found his voice.

'How did that happen?'

'What kind of question is that?'

'You always took precautions.'

'I know, but it happened anyway.'

'You're not implying it's mine?' he says. 'I haven't seen you in months.'

'You make it sound like it was back in the Ice Age. I'm saying it could be you. There's a fifty-fifty chance.'

'Okay. Have you seen a doctor? I mean, do you know for sure?'

'No, but all the obvious signs are there.'

'Before you go off the deep end, get one of those over-the-counter test kits?'

'Are you crazy? If I do, it'll be all over town.'

'Then go to the clinic in Appleton and get it done right. No one knows you there.'

'If I test positive I'll need money to get right again and I can't go to my parents. It would ruin their good opinion of me.'

'Is that what this is about? Money? You're the one who left me, remember, and now you want me to ride to your rescue like the cavalry? Shouldn't you be asking the person you left me for, the other Mr. Fifty Percent?'

'I can't. He doesn't know.'

'Don't you think it's time he does?'

'You don't understand. I can't talk to him the way I can . . . could . . . talk to you. Please help me. If you lend me the money I promise I'll pay it back.'

'I know all about your promises, Sterling.'

'I know and I'm sorry for the way I treated you. You must think I'm terrible.'

'You are terrible,' he says. 'Let me know what they say at the clinic and we'll talk again. You have to realize I'm not the same gullible guy I was before you came along.'

2

'The dog won't let me approach the body,' says Frack.

Deputy Frank 'Frack' Tilsley is first on the scene. We stand side by side in the woods at the edge of a dirt road just off the main highway. A big brown dog lies protectively over the form of a tall teenage girl. She looks like a sleeping princess in the crackling autumn grass, her hair the color of the oak leaves drifting from the tree above her head. Beneath a network of angry scratches, her face has a beautiful symmetry even in death.

I observe the dog, his labored breathing and worried eyes. 'He's scared, Frack. I'll get him some water.'

I'm Deputy Robely Danner, the only female officer on our small force. Mike, Frack and I man the substation while County Sheriff Ernie Brooker is assigned to the Coroner's Office at the county seat. Mike Oxenburg and I ride together and

Frack, the last to be hired on, usually rides solo.

I walk to the car, return with a cup of water from my thermos and kneel several paces from the dog. He's a fluffy mix, about the size of a refrigerator, who's picked up a few burrs in his double coat. He's thirsty and stressed and growls low in his throat. He licks the dead girl's cheek and nudges her hand, but she's not waking up, now or ever.

'That's a good boy,' I say. He sizes me up with a worry line between anxious eyes and runs a dry tongue between his teeth. After a moment's indecision he pulls himself to his feet and empties the cup. I check his worn leather collar but find no tags. He follows me to the car and flops down on the back seat.

My partner Mike is a big, soft-bellied teddy bear who's moving an Amish buggy and two boys on bicycles further back from the crime scene. He's a hard-working, nuts-and-bolts cop with three-year-old triplets, Tommy, Trevor and Travis, a midlife surprise for him and his wife Tammy, who works at the Stop and Go.

Frack, on the other hand, is Mike's opposite, a whippy chain-smoker with smooth muscles like steel cables. After an honorable stint in the Marines, he worked an oil fracking operation in the Dakotas before returning home. Because he's explosively powerful in a pinch, we started calling him Frack and it stuck. In last winter's white-out, he single-handedly lifted the front end of a car while I pulled a hapless passenger from beneath the undercarriage.

We're all natives of the small farming community of Abundance . . . one stop sign, two churches and three bars, one owned by my four-times divorced mother, Gladys Calhoun, whose name is all too well-known to law enforcement.

Frack and I look down on the body of the dead girl. Her blue eyes, frosted over in death, stare unblinkingly into the stratosphere. Her broken fingernails indicate a valiant struggle before someone got the best of her.

She wears jeans, a chunky pink sweater with the neck stretched down over her left shoulder and a pink and blue plaid tennis shoe on one foot. It appears to be a soft kill . . . no stab wounds, bullet holes or blood . . . but that doesn't make her any less dead. I snap photos from various angles with my camera phone and put it back in the pocket of my jacket.

'There should be another shoe around here someplace,' I say. I look at my watch. 'Forensics should be here by now. Do you know how many people trampled the scene before we got here?'

'None that I know of,' says Frack, bagging the girl's hands. 'The boys waved down the Holbeins, who put in the call from the Olsen farm. They never got out of their buggy.'

Mike motions me over and introduces me to Ty Baines and Josh Ephriam, both nine. The boys saw no suspicious activity when they stumbled onto the scene, nor do they know the girl. Mike calls Ralph Baines to pick them up.

The Holbeins' buggy sits on the shoulder of the highway. They're a young married couple named Samuel and Ruth. 'When you first arrived on the scene did you see any vehicles, anything suspicious?' I ask.

'No, just the dead girl and the two boys. Ruth found the girl's shoe in the ditch,' says Samuel. His wife hands me the shoe. She's in her early twenties with rosy cheeks and red hair tucked inside a neat black bonnet.

'Where did you find it?'

'About forty feet down the road.'

'Show me. I'll follow along.'

'Watch Lily's hooves,' he says, flicking the reins over the rump of the bay mare. 'She's still young and a bit frisky.' After a short walk Ruth points to the side of the road.

'Here?' I say.

'That's right,' she says. I climb into the ditch.

'If we're finished here,' says Samuel, 'we need to get our groceries home. If you need us, our farm is just the other side of Johnson's fruit stand.'

'Thanks for your help,' I say. 'Drive safely.' He flicks the reins and they clip-clop away.

I find two beer cans in the ditch but

they've been there a while. Deep in the weeds, a glint of light guides my hand to a tiny two-inch-long jack-knife. I brush away the dust and examine it. Two delicate and nearly illegible, letters are engraved into the silver-plate . . . E.B., B.E., or a combination thereof. It may or may not be significant. I put it in my pocket and climb back on the shoulder of the road. Above the ditch I notice where a car has skidded away the gravel.

I motion Mike over and show him. 'I think the attack started in earnest here,' I say, 'but there's no way to determine if the girl was on foot or if she'd been a passenger in the car.' I hand him the shoe and hang onto the knife as we walk back to the crime scene.

'There should be a purse somewhere, says Mike. 'My wife doesn't go anywhere without a purse.'

'Good point,' I say.

'If we don't find it it's got to be in somebody's car,' says Frack.

'You're probably right.'

A vehicle pulls into the dirt road. 'Here's the team,' says Mike, walking over to meet the coroner's van.

Frack stands at my shoulder and fires up a cigarette. He's the first man who's blipped my radar screen since my fiancé was killed during a storm three years ago. It's taken me a long time to think about moving on. Frack carries with him the scent of leather and smoke and a touch of woody aftershave. Warmth radiates through my limbs . . . and elsewhere. I step off a few paces and concentrate on the crime scene.

I was five years on the force before Frack signed on. He has a few years on me, but I have seniority on the job. He has extensive experience with firearms and I concede he's a superior shot. I've only fired my service revolver twice in the line of duty, once when a rabid raccoon got in the mayor's chicken coop and once to dispatch a wounded buck that was critically injured on the highway. I've never shot at a human being, nor had to, nor wanted to.

The forensic team gears up in white coats and rubber gloves. Frack kills his cigarette and we walk over to where Paula

Dennison, M. E., is settled on her haunches beside the body.

'Hi Paula.'

'Hi Robely. Frank.' (By the way, it's pronounced Rowblee, like row, row, row your boat.)

'What can you tell us at first glance?' I ask.

'She's dead.'

'Come on, Paula. I already figured that part out.'

She moves the girl's limbs. Mike walks over and joins us.

'You're blocking my light,' says Paula. We retreat a few steps.

'Rigor has come and gone. She's been here since sometime last night.' She takes her pen light and examines the girl's eyes. 'There's petechial hemorrhages in the whites. That's about all I can tell you with any accuracy until I complete the post-mortem.'

'So, she's been suffocated or strangled,' says Mike.

'That's a good bet. I expect to find a broken hyoid bone,' says Paula. 'Any idea who she is?'

‘Nope, not a clue,’ says Mike.

‘I doubt anyone’s missed her yet.’

‘Where’s the sheriff?’ asks Frack. ‘I thought he’d be here by now.’

‘Eddie was admitted to the hospital about an hour ago.’

‘What happened?’

‘It’s his gall bladder again. This time it comes out. He was in so much pain they took him away on a stretcher. With the sheriff out of commission, that makes you senior officer, Mike. If you need assistance you can always call the State Police.’

The crime photographer circles the body and shoots the scene from every angle using a flash in the shade cast by the trees.

‘I’m guessing she’s a high school girl or recent graduate,’ I tell Mike. ‘You want me to go through the yearbooks when we get back to the station?’

‘Good idea,’ he says. He turns to Paula. ‘How soon before we get the autopsy results?’

‘Tomorrow I’m turkey-shooting with my husband, so I’m putting this young lady on ice until Monday. As soon as I have post-mortem results I'll call. If you find out who she is, leave a message on my machine. Now get out of my hair so I can do my job.'

That's what I like about Paula. You never have to wonder what she's thinking.

3

Madison Buckley pedals her bike through a golden autumn landscape toward the Seabright farm, the leaves on the trees so bright they're hurtful to the eye. Once the last mellow day of September is torn from the calendar, the year begins its sharp decline, the sun withering around the edges like a fading sunflower.

It's hunting season, the woods and windbreaks echoing with rifle fire. Trophy bucks are strapped across fenders and hoods as hunters drive home with their bounty. Wild turkeys dance in the meadows and hundreds of miles of feed corn dry in the fields.

Madison is small and pretty, with strawberry-blonde hair and cinnamon-brown eyes. She's the kind of girl you see on feed store calendars, standing beside a wishing well with a basket of kittens on her arm. She's lost weight since her family fell on hard times and finds herself reduced to wearing patched bib overalls and worn-out shoes. A hobo bag swings from her shoulder and jingling from her wrist is a silver charm bracelet from Eddie, who left her so he could 'play the field'.

Until Sterling reappears, Madison plans to keep her parents at bay. She can't have them calling the house or driving out to the farm with a lot of questions. She flies across a narrow bridge and down the long driveway to the Seabright farmhouse.

Mr. Seabright is vacuuming the inside of his restored 1953 Buick and the hired man, Harvey Fry, is puttering with the tractor. Madison waves and walks around the house to the kitchen door. Mrs. Seabright is packing a picnic basket for their last trip to Lake Winnebago before the snow flies.

'Come in, dear,' calls Martha. Madison steps into the kitchen. 'Where's Sterling?'

'Working on her math assignment. She needs my help with long division.'

'If you and Sterling want to come to the lake this is last call. We're out of here in thirty minutes.'

'Will you be gone long?'

'We're just renting a cabin for the night.'

'That's nice,' says Madison, 'but we have to study. She sent me to pick up her Social Studies book. If we don't get off to a good start, we'll be playing catch-up for the rest of the year.'

'Be sure to tell her we want her home tomorrow in time for Mass. Four nights away from home is the limit, test or no test,' she says, putting a handful of checkered napkins in the basket, closing the lid and looking over at her daughter's best friend. 'Whatever happened to your face, dear?'

'Oh that,' says Madison, touching her cheek. 'Peterson's dog knocked me in the stickers again. I hope it doesn't look too bad.'

'Well, it doesn't look good. Be sure to put something on it so it doesn't get infected.'

Madison isn't crazy about Martha. She's sweet to her in the condescending manner well-off people reserve for those who aren't their financial equals. Madison might not be a tall, willowy blonde, but she's a much more serious student than Sterling Seabright.

'Well, go on up. You know where she keeps her stuff.'

Sterling's bedroom is furnished with a canopy bed, ruffled curtains and a shelf of basketball trophies and horse show ribbons. Displayed on the walls are her oil paintings, but they're not in the same class as Eddie Breyer's.

On a shelf is a photo of Her Majesty and Carl Hammond riding a float as last year's Pumpkin Festival Royalty. The room is a far cry from the one Madison shares with her little brother Toby, who keeps a garter snake in an aquarium and throws his dirty socks in the corner.

Madison slides her hand between the mattress and box springs, but it's too obvious a hiding place for something as important as a diary. Next she goes through the chest of drawers, feeling beneath the soft cashmere sweaters and silky slips. Nothing. She rifles the dressing table drawer. Once again she comes up empty. Where do you hide something you don't want anyone to find? She'd never leave it in her locker, so it has to be here.

'Did you find what you're looking for?' Martha calls up the staircase.

'Yes, I'll be right down,' she says, opening the closet door and running a hand over the shelf above the bar. She flips through the hangers and sees the plastic garment bag where Sterling keeps her new lavender gown. There's something hard and rectangular in the bottom. She slides down the zipper as quietly as she can.

'Madison, dear? You're holding up the show.'

'I'm coming, Mrs. Seabright.'

Madison reaches inside the garment bag and pulls out a book. It's the diary Sterling mentioned back in the summer when they were friends. When she pulls the zipper back up, the metal teeth catch in the delicate chiffon. Mrs. Seabright calls her name again so there's no time to deal with it. As she passes the dressing table she sweeps a bottle of perfume into her hobo bag, grabs the Social Studies book from the bed stand and skips down the stairs.

'Have a safe trip to the lake, Mrs. Seabright,' she calls on her way out the back door.

Martha watches from the kitchen window as Madison pedals toward the gate. She can't shake the notion that the Buckley girl is up to something. She tries to be a fair-minded Christian woman, but the Buckleys are simply not up to Seabright standards.

The car is ready to go, waxed and buffed to a mirror shine, the white walls spotless. It's going to be a lovely drive, the breeze blowing through the gold and scarlet treetops, the big car purring over the road like a contented cat.

'Come on Martha, let's go,' calls Russ.

'One minute. I want to make sure I have everything.'

'We wouldn't want to forget the kitchen sink,' he says cheerfully.

Martha goes up the stairs and looks around her daughter's room. The jewelry box is locked and in its place. There's the usual clutter of perfume bottles, lipstick tubes and fingernail polish on the dressing table and the clothes are arranged neatly in the closet. Still she senses a subtle change in the order of things.

Madison flies back over the bridge. She can't wait to get home and open the diary. Sterling has secrets and Madison is going to find out what they are.

* * *

Saturday basketball practice is held in the park above the river. Carl trots across the withered grass to the court, a slight limp reflecting the persistent pain in his groin. A cold wind blows up from the river, the team taking turns at the free throw line. Coach Breyer pulls Carl off to the side. He has an engaging personality, a pleasant round face, unruly auburn curls and a genuine interest in motivating his team both athletically and scholastically. He seems more like a big brother than an authority figure . . . just one of the guys.

'The limp is getting worse, my man,' says Coach. 'What did the doctor say?'

'Not much. He made me go to a specialist in Waupaca.'

'What kind of specialist?' It's a delicate subject. Coach means well, but he asks too many questions.

'A urologist. I thought it was a pulled muscle, but I guess it's something else.'

'What kind of something else? He's not going to sideline you is he?'

'I won't know until the lab results are in. In the meantime, I'm being reassigned to the library. No sports of any kind.'

'Okay, okay. Whatever it is, we'll deal with it. I'd hate to lose my star player, that's all. Have you heard anything else from the girl?'

'Not yet.'

'It's probably nothing then. I wouldn't stress on it.'

'That's what I'm thinking.'

'I'm always here for you, Carl. Believe it or not, I was once a teenager myself.' Coach gives him a comradely clap on the shoulder. 'Now, go back home and get off your feet.'

Carl walks away with mixed emotions. He likes Coach, but wishes he hadn't confided in him. Some things are best kept to oneself.

* * *

With Mike at the wheel we rattle across the Little Papoose River into Abundance and pull into the Stop and Go. If it weren't for the bubble-top water tower you'd hardly know the town was here. The business district is two blocks long with several 'for rent' signs in the windows, the result of a dwindling population and a crippled economy. Young people move to the city, the elderly line up for orchestra seats at the local cemetery and rock-bottom prices at Walmart in New London lure customers away from local shops.

Abundance is small enough that everyone knows who gets DWIs or qualifies for food stamps, and big enough to have a right side and a wrong side of the tracks. On the right side are big, Victorian houses with giant shade trees, and on the wrong side is the trailer court, the dump and Buba's Biker Bar.

Tammy tells Mike that she'll pick up the triplets at daycare and bring home a couple frozen pizzas for dinner. I watch him set chocolate milk and a bag of potato chips on the counter. In the last hour his face has become uncharacteristically red and blotchy. I chalk it up to a stressful morning and a cold wind. I buy a bag of cheese curds, a sack of dry dog food and two scratch-offs.

When we arrive at the station Mike goes to work on his report. No calls have come in about a missing girl. The dog lies down beside my desk and I start looking through the yearbooks while Frack is sent to break up a dispute at the trailer park over ownership of a 20-year-old automobile sitting on blocks.

Sherry Mendel, our civilian dispatcher, swivels her chair in my direction. She's cute and perky with a head of bouncy, honey-colored curls. 'What is that big brown thing on the floor?' she says. 'When he snores he sounds like my husband Henry.'

'For now he's Fargo,' I say, naming him after my favorite movie. I tell her how he stood vigil over the dead girl.

'If you find out who the dog belongs to, it might lead to the girl's identity,' she says.

'That's what I was thinking. I'll start by showing him to the crowd at Gladys's tonight.'

I spend the next half hour scouring the yearbooks for a photo of our victim. Wisconsin is full of natural blondes, evidenced by the ethnic groups that settled its towns: Scandinavia, Rhinelander, Berlin, Demark and two German towns. In Abundance there's a sizeable Danish and German population.

I check the yearbook photos against the ones on my camera-phone and see no matches among last year's graduating seniors. This year's book won't be out until the end of the year. Finally, a girl on last year's junior basketball team looks like a possibility. She's photographed in profile, a gold braid flying, her body two and a half feet off the floor as she sinks a ball through the hoop. I run the photo by Sherry.

'You have a girl in high school,' I say. 'Do you know who this girl is, the one making the basket?'

'It's hard to tell from that angle, but it could be Sterling Seabright. They say she's a good enough player to give the boys a run for their money. Her family owns an upscale dairy farm on Cloverdale Cut. If you want to run out there I'll watch his lordship,' she says, nodding toward the dog.

'I think I will. I owe you one.'

'Two,' she says with a laugh.

'Let me run it by Mike and see what he thinks.'

'Don't forget my vacation starts tomorrow,' says Sherry.

'I did forget. You guys going hunting?'

'If there's anything I hate, it's bullets and blood. We're going to Miami Beach to get a sunburn and drink pina coladas.'

'I am so jealous. Drink one for me.'

'Two,' she says. I give her a thumbs up.

Mike sits listlessly at his desk staring at the computer screen, his hands stalled above the keyboard. He looks feverish and disoriented.

'Anything wrong, Mike?'

'I'm dizzy and my ears are ringing like

church bells. I don't know what's wrong with me. One thing's for sure, I'm not getting anywhere on my report.'

'Did you get your shot this year? They're predicting a bad flu season.'

'I got one last year,' he says, sheepishly.

'You know that's not good enough. Go home, Big Bear. You're coming down with something. I'm going to check out a lead, then I'll type up your report.'

'You sure?'

'You bet.'

'I hate to flake on you, especially with Ernie in the hospital.'

'If you don't get out of here, we're all going to be in the hospital.'

'You're right.' He stands and puts a hand on the desk to get his bearings.

'I'll call Tammy and tell her you're on your way home. Are you okay to drive?'

'I'll be fine. It's the walking I have trouble with.'

* * *

I cross the bridge and park in front of the closed gate on Cloverdale Cut. The

Seabrights have quite an operation: a fine herd of Brown Swiss, a big white house and well-maintained outbuildings. There's a red tractor in front of the barn and a green John Deere near the house. A quality Arabian mare is frolicking along the fence line.

I give my siren a few short chirps and set the light bar flashing. As soon as I see a man emerge from the barn I turn off the lights. He climbs on the mower and drives in my direction.

'What can I do for you?' he says, getting off the machine and approaching the gate. He's fiftyish with stooped posture and thinning brown hair.

'I'm Deputy Danner. Are you Mr. Seabright?' I ask.

'I'm Harvey Fry, the hired help,' he says, resting his arms on the top of the gate. 'The Seabrights are up to the lake for the night, but they'll be back tomorrow.'

'Do they have a daughter named Sterling?'

'They do.'

'Is she with them?'

'No, she's staying with a friend for a few days.'

'When did you see her last?'

'Oh, let me think. That would be Wednesday when she drove off to school. Why, is something wrong?'

'What was she driving?'

'A new Kia Soul. Alien green.'

'Alien green?'

'It's what we used to call chartreuse, but everything's got to have a fancy name these days. You can see it coming for a mile. Did you find her stolen saddle? Is that what this is about?'

'I just need a word with her. Do you know the name of the girl she's with?'

'I've heard it, but I don't have a memory for names. She came to the house earlier in the day to pick up a text book.'

'Her friend?'

'Yes.'

'And Miss Seabright wasn't with her?'

'That's right.'

'Do you know where she lives?'

'On a farm I would imagine.'

That certainly narrows it down.

'If you want to leave your card, I'll have someone call you. They paid over a thousand dollars for that saddle. It got swiped from the tack room at the fairgrounds.'

I hand him my card, my cell phone number scribbled on the back. The photo can wait until I get a better grip on the situation. Besides, if Sterling is with her friend today, she's not the girl in the woods. Nevertheless, I'd feel better if her family had seen her since Wednesday.

4

Madison leans her bike against the barn and goes inside. Sunlight slices between the boards as she climbs the ladder to the loft and leans back against a bale of hay.

Wednesday was the first time Sterling had spoken to her since mid-summer.

'*Can I tell Mom I'm staying with you for a few days?*' she asked.

'*I don't know. Until when?*'

'*I'll be back on Sunday and tell you everything.*' Sterling touched her arm and smiled her warm, blue-eyed smile. It was almost like they were best friends again.

That of course, was before she caught Sterling at Eddie's and lost her temper.

Madison digs in her bag and tosses the school book aside. She removes the flared glass stopper from the perfume bottle and breathes in the warm, spicy scent. She shouldn't have let her jealousy get the best of her. It would have been smarter if she'd waited until Sunday to hear what

Sterling had to say.

She returns the fancy bottle to the bag and removes the diary. It's cloth-covered in a bright geometric design, one of those blank-page books you get in fancy bookstores. She flips randomly through the pages, reminded of the happy days of June and Eddie. July. Sterling describes her as clever and fun to be with, memorializing their carefree days of riding horses and skinny-dipping in the Blue Hole back in the woods. They spent three days at The Dells with Sterling's parents that summer, carried a 6-pack down to the river and got buzzed beneath the stars. Then around mid-July the Seabrights bought Sterling a car and everything changed. She was always out, didn't accept or return calls and never returned to the Blue Hole.

Madison turns to the second week of their senior year.

Today when Social Studies let out I only had a few minutes before math class. I wanted to be alone, but Madison was right behind me, stuck to my sweater like a burr. She dropped her book and I made my escape when she bent to pick it up. I caught Carl coming out of Biology.

Madison could never understand Sterling breaking up with the nicest boy in school. Carl was tall, blond and movie-star handsome. Every girl wanted to win him and every guy wanted to be him.

We stood at his locker. I'd dumped him without explanation so he's not overjoyed to see me. I barely open my mouth when I'm jostled from behind. I turn around and it's HER! I wonder how long she's been standing there. 'Do you mind?' I snapped. She looks hurt, fails to understand I'm no longer the girl I was at the Blue Hole. 'I'll see you at lunchtime,' I tell her. I see a tear and a flash of controlled anger in her face. I walk away from them both. At lunchtime I sit with my team mates. I don't want to deal with Madison's feelings. I have enough trouble dealing with my own.

'Madison Diane Buckley! Where are you hiding?' Mom steps into the barn, a scarf tied in a bow on her forehead like Rosie the Riveter.

'I'm up here studying, Mom.'

'You can do that later. I've made you a peanut butter and jelly sandwich, then I want you to rake out the goat shed.'

She has to keep her grades up. A full scholarship is her only ticket out of Abundance. She never wants to see another goat or eat another peanut butter and jelly sandwich.

* * *

Gladys's Bar sits in the mosquito zone on the west bank of the Little Papoose River. It's built of split logs with a green beer sign flickering in the window. The walls are hung with mounted deer trophies, antique guns and Fox Indian artefacts. When you walk in, the first thing you see through the smoke is the No Smoking sign mounted above the cash register. Gladys keeps a Derringer in the cash drawer, a baseball bat behind the bar and is proficient in the use of both.

Gladys's is a popular establishment, frequented by men in jeans and work boots, the girls in tighter jeans, discrete tattoos of roses and butterflies inked on their ankles and shoulders. Most of the customers are regulars, the same faces week after week, year after year, until they go off to that big brewery in the sky.

The sounds are the sounds of my childhood: leather dice cups slapping against the bar, the ding of a 1940s pinball machine, the click of balls on the pool table and the cha-chunk as packs of cigarettes tumble from the machine into the tray. A Worlitzer bubbles red and blue beside a rear window overlooking the river.

I enter on a blast of cold air, a big bag of kibble in my arms and Fargo trotting at my heels. Gladys gives me a nod as she slides a beer to a man down the bar. My mother is fiftyish, but looks about sixty-five. She has dyed red hair and a complexion pickled and smoked from a lifetime of alcohol and cigarette use. That doesn't mean that a certain kind of man (like the four she married and divorced) doesn't find her husky voice and pre-cancerous cough irresistibly sexy.

Fargo draws an instant crowd. A man with a big handlebar mustache takes out a hunting knife and cuts the burrs from his coat. A girl in a blue topped-off tank sets a saucer of beer in front of him and watches him lap it up . . . the dog, not the lumberjack.

I walk to the bar and plunk the dog food at my feet. On the back wall is a photo of me and my late fiancé, Australian-born David McClorry. We're astride his death machine in our happy days before the fast bike met the slow tractor.

'I could use a saucer of beer myself,' I say, climbing on a stool.

'Where did the Shetland pony come from?' says Gladys.

She pours me a cold one and I tell her about Fargo and the dead girl. I pass my phone through the room. A trucker says he saw the dog sitting on the shoulder of the highway a few days back. A woman in a cowboy hat says the blonde looks like a masseuse who moved to Hollywood a couple years ago.

After two more beers I climb the stairs to my room above the bar. Like me, Fargo has had one too many, trips on a step and hits his chin on the landing. I tug his collar to keep him from falling asleep on the stairs. I shift the dog food bag to my left arm, insert the key in my door and find it unlocked.

The folks at Gladys's are too often the ones I pick up on petty thievery and bad checks, so I religiously keep my door locked. I push it open, snap on the light and set the bag inside with a thump. Someone has been in my room, some *two* actually, given the odor of cheap cologne and sweaty funk. My bedspread is mangled, a black cigarette burn near the pillows. An ashtray beside the bed contains eight butts, three smeared with bright red lipstick.

The curtains smell like stale cigarette smoke. I raise the window with an angry clack, letting the night wind sweep the room. When I turn around Fargo is sleeping at the foot of the bed. Vibrating with indignation, I grab the ashtray, trot back downstairs and slam it on the bar.

'What?' says Gladys, with a startled look on her face.

'Who did you let inside my room?'

'Just Jackie and Howie, hon. They got

into a brouhaha. I couldn't have them upsetting all the customers.'

'Then you kick their butts out the door, not upstairs to my room. I pay my rent and it's not like this is the first time you've invaded my privacy.'

'I'm so so-o-orry. I didn't think you'd notice.'

'You didn't what? They were up there long enough to smoke eight cigarettes and burn a hole in my bedspread. If you're so magnanimous, let them camp in your room!'

'You know I can't do that, hon. The bank bag is in there.'

'Oh great, why don't you shout it through a megaphone? I should . . . '

'What?' she laughs. 'Call a cop?'

'Give me your key,' I say, my hand trembling with anger.

'That's the only one I have. What if there's a fire and I have to get into your room?'

'You let the building burn down and collect the insurance. Now give.' She reaches in her pocket and drops the key in my palm. 'Thank you. You can have it back in a few days when I move out.'

5

'Wasn't that a lovely drive?' says Martha, as Russ sets the luggage inside the door. 'The season's last golden breath. The Andersens will make sure we get the same cabin next summer, the one with the shower *and* the tub.'

'Every time we go to the lake, someone's missing. Have you noticed that, Martha? Last year it was Joe Pendergast carried off by cancer,' says Russ. 'This year lupus took Edith Corwin.'

'The older we get the more I think we should sell the farm after Sterling goes off to college. I'm tired of winter. It gets longer and colder every year. We could move to Florida like the Freemans.'

'I can't say the thought hasn't crossed my mind. It's not like we haven't had offers from those big conglomerates.'

Martha moves the curtain aside and looks out the picture window. 'I don't see

Sterling's car. I thought she'd be back by now. I wonder if the Buckley girl passed along my message.'

'Attending church with her parents isn't exactly the high point of her social calendar. I wouldn't go myself if you didn't drag me there by the ring in my nose.'

'Oh Russ,' she says with a laugh. 'It can't be that bad. Imagine what it was like in Grandma Jansen's day with everything in Latin.'

'Heaven forbid.' Russ picks up a business card from the coffee table. 'What have we here? It's from that lady sheriff with the odd name. She's written her cell phone number on the back.'

'It'll be about the saddle. I'm too tired to deal with it today. I'm calling the Buckleys to touch base with Sterling,' she says, picking up the phone and punching in the number. She listens for a moment and clicks off. 'For heaven's sake! I got a recording. *The number you have dialed is not receiving calls at this time*. Knowing them, they haven't paid their bill.'

'Don't be too hard on them, Martha.

They're not the only ones affected by the economy.' He stretches and works a kink out of his back. 'I'm hungry. I want to finish off that chocolate cake in the fridge. All that driving has got my sciatica acting up. I don't feel like sitting for an hour on a hard church bench, do you?'

'Not really. See if you can find a good movie on TV, while I get into something comfortable,' she says, giving him a peck on the cheek.

'How about we turn off the ringer and have a *real* day of rest?'

* * *

I open my eyes as sunlight slides under the window shade. There's nothing quieter than a bar on Sunday morning unless it's midnight in a cemetery. Fargo has abandoned his spot on the floor and fallen asleep with his head on the pillow next to mine. Because he outweighs me, he feels entitled to more than half the bed. Only seems fair, right?

I run my hand over his massive head. 'Good morning, Fargo.'

He opens his eyes and rests his chin on my shoulder.

'You have beer breath,' I say. He thumps his tail happily. I swing my legs over the edge of the bed and finger-comb my layered shag of chestnut brown hair. My hair is no-nonsense, like most of my clothes . . . wash, dry and fly.

The boys and I work Sundays on rotation, but with Eddie in the hospital and Mike sick in bed, I'm lead officer on what I've tagged The Blonde Beauty Case. There will be no lying in bed reading Fargo the funny papers. I feed and water the dog, shower and dress and take him for a walk along the river. When he's done his business we pile into the pickup and drive to the Stop and Go. Tammy says Mike has a roaring case of the flu and could be down for a week or more. I promise that I'll keep him updated. I buy coffee and a bear claw. Fargo eats the bear and leaves me the claw.

Frack and I pull into the station at the same time. I stay to make some calls and he leaves to canvas the households within a mile of the crime scene, hoping someone might have seen or heard something the night of the homicide. I get no answer at the Seabright residence and figure they've gone on to church. By mid-afternoon, still unable to reach them, I wonder if they've stayed on at the lake. I drum my fingers on the desk and call the residence of the high school principal, Neville Gregory. His wife Caroline picks up.

'This is Robely down at the station, Caroline. Is Neville around this morning?'

'I'm sorry, he's gone north for the weekend, but I expect him home later this evening.'

'Wild turkey or deer?' I ask.

'It's deer this time. Thank god, he's a terrible shot. There's nothing I hate more than walking into the garage and bumping into a deer hanging upside down from the rafters. Is there anything I can help you with?'

'Not really. He has my cell phone number. Have him call me if he gets in before nine or so, otherwise I'll call him at school in the morning.'

In the case of a missing person I'd run off flyers, tack them on telephone poles, run the photo in the press and pass them out to businesses, but what I have is a body and a missing family. I can't very well plaster the town with photos of the homicide scene.

I tap my fingers on the desk, drink too much coffee, and pace up and down the empty office waiting for a call that never comes. The town is virtually closed down on Sundays or I'd be canvasing the shops and asking questions. I continue to call the Seabrights throughout the afternoon, but no one picks up.

I try looking at the case from another perspective. It's possible the victim is older than I think, in her early twenties and living on her own. If she works and has no roommate or significant other, she might not be missed until Monday. It's also possible she's not local. She could be a hitchhiker from another town or another state. Several years ago a woman was murdered in Chicago and her body dumped in the snow near Racine.

At the end of the day not one call has come into the station, nor has Frack unearthed a single viable clue. No one living near the murder scene had noticed anything out of the ordinary that night. I leave my cell phone number with the 911 operator, lock up and go home. I climb the back stairs to my room to avoid getting into it with Gladys again. I change into jeans, a red angora sweater and penny loafers, then slip my silver and turquoise bracelet on my wrist, grab my jean jacket, whistle to Fargo and head out the door.

Unable to get the case off my mind, I return to the crime scene looking for a missed clue among the leaves, a message written in the clouds, an epiphany on the wind, anything to point me in the right direction. I find Frack beneath the oak tree in a leather jacket and high-top boots, his pickup parked at the edge of the field. I step under the crime tape. Fargo lies down in the shriveled grass and puts his chin on his paws.

'Hi beautiful,' says Frack.

'That's Deputy Beautiful to you,' I say

with a smile. 'Did the team miss anything?'

'I don't think so. I've walked the area a dozen times. A wallet with an I.D. would have been nice.' A cold wind whips through my hair and I give a little shiver. Frack casually pulls me against him, the back of my head resting lightly on his chest.

'You feel so damn good,' he says. 'Want a cigarette?'

'You can look at Gladys and ask me that?'

'You couldn't look like Gladys if you smoked three packs a day.'

'I'll take that as a compliment . . . sort of. It's official. Mike's got the flu. He won't be back for days.'

'Tammy told me when I went in for a Lotto ticket. I guess we're partnered up on this one.' He gently picks an oak leaf out of my hair. 'I can't have a little girl alone out there with a murderer on the loose.'

'Don't start with me.'

Frack's leather and tobacco smell is comforting. It makes me feel safe and taken care of. I can't remember what my father looked like, but I remember his scent: leather, cigarette smoke, pine trees. People who knew him say he was a nice man, a big French-Canadian from Quebec Province. I've been told little about him except he's the only man my mother didn't marry, sticking me with Gladys's maiden name. I once asked her why they never married. She said he wanted her to change her ways and that ended the relationship. I want her to change her ways too, but it's not going to happen.

'Do you realize we're dispatched to forty or fifty accidents for every murder?' I say. 'This is the first murder-mystery I've been assigned to and we're down two men.'

'What do you mean, the first?'

'Five years ago Ellie Fisher shot her abusive husband while he was sleeping. When we walked in she was sitting at the kitchen table with the gun in front of her. Six months later Herbert Henderson killed Roger Dooley in a bar fight. He had a knife in his hand

and blood on his clothes. Then there was that wacky old woman who ran her grown son down with a tractor because he wouldn't drive her to her Bible study group. None of them were whodunits.'

'You're right. I guess we can't phone this one in.'

'Speak for yourself,' I say, giving him a nudge.

Smoke from his cigarette trails off in the wind and I feel his warm breath in my hair.

'You sure smell good,' he says.

'It's coconut shampoo from the Dollar Store,' I tell him. A dust devil sends the fallen leaves somersaulting through the air. 'I'm keeping Fargo if he goes unclaimed, but I'm still hoping he leads us to the identity of the victim. We've done everything we can until the town opens up tomorrow.'

'I don't know what's wrong with people around here. They think Sunday is for family and church,' he jokes, giving me a little squeeze. Wind ruffles my hair and I open my eyes.

'Makes it hard to get anything done. I'm going to the high school in the morning with the girl's photo. You wanna come?'

'Sure,' he says. 'You wanna to go for a drink tonight?'

I take a long moment to decide.

'Not to Gladys's,' I say. 'We're not on friendly terms at the moment. I'm moving out.'

'No kidding. You got a place lined up?'

'Not yet.'

'I'll keep my ear to the ground. Of course there's always my extra bed . . . '

'No, don't even go there.'

'How about we hit The Edge of Town? We can take a quiet booth in the back and go over the case.'

'Okay. And don't look at me like that. This is a work date, not a roll in the hay.'

'Come on. Look me in the eye. Tell me you don't want to.'

'Don't want to what?'

'You know.' He smiles his most captivating smile, the kind designed to soften my resolve and melt my armor like warm candle wax. I go a little weak in the knees and can't help smiling back.

'Frack, if I did everything I wanted to do, I'd weigh three hundred pounds and be in jail for matricide.'

6

Monday morning breaks crisp and clear with leaves whirling across the fields and a sky of serious, ceramic blue. Russ Seabright heads down the long drive to the mailbox. Sahara Star whinnies and follows him along the fence until she gets the apple in the pocket of his robe. Now that he's successful enough to employ Harvey and a couple young farm hands, he no longer has to wrestle with the milking machines at 5 a.m. He gathers the mail and heads back to the house.

He slides into the breakfast nook across from Martha and sorts through the mail, putting the catalogues aside for later. 'Here's something from the school,' he says. 'You want to open it?'

'You go ahead,' says Martha, blowing on her coffee cup. He uses his letter opener and makes a clean cut beneath the flap of the envelope. Inside is a brief message beneath the Abundance High

School letterhead. He finishes reading and looks at Martha with a bewildered expression on his face. 'What is it, dear?'

'A truancy notice.'

Martha laughs out loud. 'Sterling's never been truant. She's never even been tardy.'

'It says she hasn't been in attendance since last Wednesday. That's almost a week ago.'

She adjusts her bifocals and sets the morning paper aside. 'Let me see that.' She reads it twice. 'This can't be right.'

'You don't think the girls have been cutting class, do you?'

'It would certainly be out of character for Sterling. As for the Buckley girl, nothing would surprise me.'

'I'm calling the school and getting this straightened out,' says Russ.

Martha sets her cup in the saucer with a click. 'I'm getting dressed. This warrants a face to face.' Fifteen minutes later she's pinning an amber broach on the front of her new autumn suit. Russ steps into the doorway of the bedroom as she collects her gloves and purse.

'She's not there,' he says.

'What do you mean? It's Monday. She has to be there.'

'But, she's not.' Martha notices the tremor in Russ's right hand that appears only when he's under stress.

'What about Madison Buckley?'

'They won't tell me, but Mr. Gregory will see us as soon as we arrive.'

⋆ ⋆ ⋆

Frack and I meet at the station early Monday morning.

'Where's the beast?' he says.

'In bed. He's not a morning person. If he eats the chest of drawers, I'll come up with another plan.'

The phone rings. It's Paula.

'Morning, Robely. Is Mike in?' she says.

'You're stuck with me and Frank, Paula. Mike is down with the flu.' I put her on speaker.

'I came in early and did the post-mortem on the girl,' she says. 'Any I.D. yet?'

'Not yet, but if she's local we hope to

know something by the end of the day.'

'Okay, here we go. Caucasian female, sixteen to twenty years old. Five ten and a half. One hundred and fifteen pounds. Estimated time of death: eleven p.m. on Friday to three a.m. on Saturday. Cause of death: strangulation. Manner of death: homicide. No drugs or alcohol in her system. The hyoid bone was broken as was her right radius.'

'Her arm?' I say.

'Yes, the shorter, thicker of the two bones below the elbow. Probably a defensive wound. There was no evidence of sexual assault, but that doesn't mean it wasn't a crime of sexual aggression. Now, for a couple of surprises. The scratches on her face were acquired twenty-four, maybe forty-eight hours before death.'

'She'd been held hostage?' says Frack.

'Good guess, but if that were the case, I'd expect to find tape residue or ligature marks on her wrists or ankles and neither were present. It looks like she'd been in an altercation a day or two before her murder.'

'Seems like there was a lot going on in this girl's life.'

'I'm just getting warmed up,' says Paula. 'Although the victim was outwardly healthy, tall and muscularly fit, her abnormally low weight and minimal body fat raise a red flag. Her hip and pelvic bones protruded. You could count her ribs. It's the kind of unhealthy body image we see in athletes and runway models. It too often passes for glamour in our society and therefore isn't always recognized or taken seriously.'

'You mean anorexia?' I say.

'That's right. If this were New York or L.A., I'd swear she was a runway model.'

'How about a basketball player.'

'That would fit. I suspect our victim suffered from amenorrhea,' says Paula. 'Excessive exercise and low calorie intake leads to a deficiency of the hormones ghrelin and leptin, resulting in low bone density and the cessation of menstruation. A bone scan confirmed my suspicions. Her bones would have broken more easily than the average person her age.'

'That all very interesting,' I say, 'but what bearing does it have on our case?'

'Think, Robely. Young, fertile, no period. What does that suggest to you?'

'Pregnancy.'

'She may have *thought* she was pregnant, but she wasn't.'

'If she thought so, that means she was sexually active,' I say.

'There you go. I sent fingernail scraping to the lab for DNA, but it will be months before we get results.'

'Let's hope we have this solved a lot sooner than that. Thank you, Paula. Anything else?'

'That's it. Talk to you later.' She hangs up.

'If she thought she was pregnant, she'd know who got her that way,' says Frack.

'Could be a he or a them,' I say. 'Now, we're talking motive.'

I check my watch. 'Mr. Gregory is in a powwow with the Superintendent of Schools, but he has us penciled in for eleven. If we don't have an I.D. by the end of the day, we'll go public. I'm surprised the news of her death hasn't already leaked out. We don't know that the girl is from Abundance, only that she was murdered and dumped in Waupaca County. And where does the dog fit in?'

'Beats me. The Seabrights have my card. If they were missing a dog they'd have called. If they were missing a daughter they'd have called sooner.'

'Unless, they don't know they're missing.'

At ten thirty the phone rings. I listen for about a minute. 'Don't touch anything else until we get there,' I say, and hang up. 'That was Gayle Shipley. A green Kia was parked behind her hardware store when she opened on Saturday morning. When it was still there this morning, she became concerned. It was unlocked and the keys were under the floor mat. It's registered to Russell Seabright.'

'Now we're cookin',' says Frack, grabbing his jacket.

The hardware store is one block up Main from the station. A minute later we swing into the back alley. Gayle is standing beside the car with a pencil behind her ear, wearing a cotton smock with big pockets. She hands me the car keys. Leaving houses and cars unlocked in these small farming communities is not unusual.

'I thought someone had car trouble,' says Gayle, 'but the tank is half full and it starts right up without a stutter. Everyone knows these spaces are for the Amish on Saturday, so when it was still here this morning I knew something wasn't right.'

'Did you move the seat when you got in?' asks Frack.

'All I did was start it and check the registration in the glove box to see who owned it.'

'The seat's pushed way back to accommodate someone of greater than average height,' says Frack.

'Let's get it dusted for prints,' I say.

'What's going on?' says Gayle.

'We're trying to figure that out,' I tell her.

A customer steps out the back door with a socket set in one hand and his wallet in the other.

'Hey Gayle, you want my money or not?'

'Gotta go,' she says.

'When the print team is through can they leave the keys with you so the owner can pick up the car?'

'Sure, that's fine.'

The car's interior is pristine, no fast food wrappers on the floor, no cigarette butts in the ashtray. In the glove box is the registration, a couple maps and a roll of breath mints. There's not so much as a stray penny or lost earring under the seats. We open the trunk and find a spare, a jack, a jug of anti-freeze, five cans of oil, a flashlight and the kind of insulated blanket people carry in case they get stranded in the snow.

'Looks like she was prepared for every eventuality,' I say.

'Except the one that got her dead,' says Frack. After we brief the print team, we head for the school, twenty minutes late for our appointment. 'There were no obvious signs of struggle in that car.'

'If she was grabbed I don't think she'd have found time to put the key under the mat.'

'She left the car voluntarily and

planned to return Friday night or Saturday morning before the buggies arrived,' he says. 'Then something came up.'

'Something like murder.'

7

Carl should have kept his problems to himself, even though he never mentioned Sterling by name. He goes to the gym before class in hope of undoing the damage and finds Coach alone on the court.

'Can I have a word?'

'Sure Carl, what's on your mind?' he says, dribbling the ball to the edge of the court.

'It's about what I told you a while back. Turns out it was a false alarm.'

'Are you sure?'

'One hundred percent.'

'Well, that's good. I don't want you jeopardizing your college scholarship. You'll be a damn good coach in your own right if you stop letting pretty girls turn your head.' Carl hopes to one day go into medical research, but lets the coach believe what he will.

'I hope you haven't mentioned this to anyone.'

'Mention what? I've already forgotten what we were talking about,' he says, sinking the ball from twenty feet away.

'By the way, I hear you're trying to get one of the girls on our team. You really think Abundance is ready for that?'

'You mean the Seabright girl? She's been riding me about it, but when I ran it by Gregory, you'd think I was trying to put her on the front lines in Afghanistan.'

Carl laughs. 'I can imagine. Besides, Miss Lunn would have a fit if you stole her star athlete.'

'You used to go with her, didn't you?' he says, recapturing the ball and bouncing it in place.

'That's ancient history. I guess I wasn't her type.'

'She seeing someone else now?' There he goes with the questions again.

'Who knows? It's not like we talk anymore.' Carl sees the time on the wall clock. 'I have to get going if I want to make my doctor's appointment.'

* * *

Alice Markham sits behind Madison in Algebra, but instead of paying attention to Mrs. Frankel, she's watching maple leaves drift past the window and thinking about piercing her nose and dying a purple stripe in her hair. She leans forward and pokes Madison in the back with a pencil.

'What?' says Madison, twitching her shoulder. 'I'm trying to concentrate.'

'Well, concentrate on this. A patrol car just pulled to the curb. It's the lady cop and that hot Frank Tilsley.' Madison looks out the window. 'Do you think they're getting it on? I would be if I were her.'

'Alice, would you please shut up!'

Alice slumps back with a pout. 'Are you ever touchy this morning.'

The deputies get out of their vehicle and walk toward the main entrance. A sudden tightening in Madison's diaphragm makes it hard to catch her breath.

'What do you think is going on?' whispers Alice, unable to contain herself. 'I bet that boy from the trailer park was smoking weed in the restroom again.'

Ten minutes later the Seabrights' Buick pulls into the lot and Madison is gripped by panic. She knew that Sterling wouldn't show on Sunday because of their fight, but now it's Monday and she's not in school. The first thing the Seabrights will do is come looking for her. The room slips out of focus. Sweat breaks out on her forehead and she's overcome by a dizzying swirl of nausea. She grabs her books and rushes to the front of the room.

'Mrs. Frankel, I'm going to throw up,' she says.

'Go straight to the nurse's office,' says Mrs. Frankel. 'I'll call ahead and let them know you're coming.'

* * *

Mr. Gregory stands when Frack and I enter his office.

'Hello, Robely. Frank. Take the load off,' he says, pointing at the chairs in front of his desk.

'How was your hunting trip?' I ask.

'I went with a few friends to my

brother's hunting lodge. We had a grand time.'

'Bag anything this year?'

'Tri-tip and beer. It's an excuse to get away from the gals.'

'So that's why Caroline thinks you're a bad shot.'

'You won't give us away will you?'

'Your secret is safe with us,' I say.

He taps his pen on the blotter. 'So, what can I do for you today? Has one of my students gotten himself in trouble?'

'I'm afraid it's more serious than that, Neville. Do you have a student enrolled named Sterling Seabright?'

'Yes, she's a senior this year, but she's been uncharacteristically truant since last week. Her parents are coming in for a conference this morning. I hope she hasn't done something foolish like elope.'

'A dead girl was found about seven miles outside of town on Saturday. Tall. Blonde. Late teens.'

'Certainly you don't think it's her?'

'We're not sure. That's one reason we've come to you. Her car has been sitting behind the hardware store for a few days,' says Frack, 'and we've been unable to reach the Seabrights. Are you up to looking at a photo taken at the scene?'

'You mean of the dead girl?'

'Yes.'

'I suppose,' he says, reluctantly. I bring the photo up and pass the phone across the desk. Gregory takes a deep breath and barely glances at it before passing it back.

'Yes, I believe that's her.'

'That wasn't much of a look, Neville. Are you sure?'

'I'm sure I've seen her in the pink sweater. Was it a riding accident?'

'She was the victim of homicide,' says Frack. 'She was strangled.'

'You're saying she was murdered? That's impossible! She was one of our most popular students.'

'Can you think of any reason someone would want her dead?'

'No, of course not! She was well-liked, a star athlete.'

'How about boyfriends or ex-boyfriends?'

'Last year she went steady with a boy named Carl Hammond, but they're not together this year.'

I write the name down. 'What's he like?'

'He's well-regarded. From a good family. His father's been employed at Hillshire Farms for fifteen years. His mother is a manager at the Walmart in New London. The boy has never been in any kind of trouble.'

'Do you know if it was an amiable break-up?' I ask. 'Those things can get pretty intense.'

'I wouldn't know.'

'Had she mentioned having problems with anyone? Rivalries? Someone with a less than healthy interest in her? That sort of thing.'

'If she did, that information never reached my desk, so it couldn't have been anything serious.' He leans forward with an earnest look on his face. 'I can't imagine anyone from Abundance doing something like this.'

'We've only started working the case,' I say. 'It's customary to start with the people she associated most closely with. If she shared a confidence with someone, who do you think it would be?'

'I have no idea. I suggest you talk with her teachers or her classmates. I'll have Mrs. Finch provide you with her schedule.'

'Thank you. That would be helpful,' I say.

The intercom buzzes and he presses the button.

'Yes, Mrs. Finch.'

'The Seabrights are here about their daughter, Mr. Gregory.'

He runs a hand over his bald spot. 'I can't do this,' he says. 'I don't know what to say.'

Frack and I are already standing. 'We'll take over from here,' I say. 'Thank you for seeing us on such short notice.'

8

Neville leaves Frack and me at a table in the conference room with the Seabrights. Russ is the kind of man who opens doors for his wife, drives her to DAR meetings and hair appointments. Martha wears a nicely-tailored suit and kid gloves. Introductions are made. She fidgets with the clasp of her purse. He has a noticeable tremor in his hand.

'Where's Mr. Gregory?' he asks. 'What are you two doing here?'

'Mr. Seabright . . . ' I begin.

'Tell us what's going on. This can't be about our daughter's truancy.'

'I'm afraid it's a much more serious matter. You need to brace yourself for bad news.'

'Oh, Russ,' says Martha. He gives her hand a reassuring pat.

'What kind of bad news are we talking about?' he says.

'Your daughter is deceased,' I tell him.

'We're very sorry to be the bearers of such bad news.'

For a moment time stands still.

'Deceased?' says Martha softly, like she's hearing the word for the first time and its meaning is unclear.

'She was found in the woods a few miles from town about one o'clock on Saturday.'

'That's impossible,' says Martha. 'It has to be someone who looks like her.'

'Mr. Gregory viewed a photo taken at the scene. She was wearing a pink sweater and pink and blue tennis shoes.'

She presses gloved fingers to her mouth. Russ looks at Frack. 'Are you telling us there's been some kind of an accident?'

'She was the victim of homicide, Mr. Seabright.'

'Homicide? You can't mean murder?' says Russ.

'Yes, I'm afraid that's the case.'

'Do you have the person who did this?'

'Not yet,' says Frack.

'Do you know who did it?'

'Not yet, but we will,' I say.

I scroll up the photo. 'This picture was taken at the scene if you're prepared to look at it, Mr. Seabright.'

Russ pauses, then takes it from my hand. Martha turns her eyes away. He takes his time looking for evidence to distance himself from an unacceptable truth. When he hands back the phone I see the resignation on his face.

'Yes, that's her. That's Sterling,' he says.

'Oh, Russ, no,' says Martha in a soft voice. She sits silently for a long moment, then leans purposely forward in her chair, relief sweeping her face. 'Wait a minute. Just wait. Something's not right here. You say this girl was found on Saturday?'

'Yes, Mrs. Seabright, on Saturday,' I say.

'It can't be her then, don't you see? There's been some terrible mix-up. She was alive Saturday afternoon when her friend came by to pick up a school book. They were studying together that day. You can check. Her name is Madison. Madison Buckley. They have a farm on Berry Creek Road. Sterling has been staying there for a few days. All you have to do is make one call and this whole matter can be cleared up.'

Madison Buckley. I write the name down.

'When was the last time you actually laid eyes on your daughter?' I ask.

'It was last Wednesday morning, wasn't it Russ?'

'Yes, dear.'

'Mrs. Seabright, the Buckley girl was . . . uninformed,' I say. 'By the time she came by the farm, your daughter had been deceased for over twelve hours. She died sometime around midnight on Friday or shortly thereafter.'

'But, don't you see? That makes no sense at all.'

'Please, Martha,' says Russ, touching her gloved hand and slowly shaking his head. 'It's her. It's Sterling, my dear.'

'I don't understand,' she says, blinking away tears. 'If she and Madison weren't studying together, why pick up the book?'

Russ turns to his wife. 'I'm going to drop you off when we're through here and then I'm going straight to the

Buckleys and find out for myself what's going on.'

'That would be counterproductive, Mr. Seabright,' says Frack. 'You'll only impede our investigation. We'll be speaking with Miss Buckley ourselves. It's important we do everything by the book.'

'I suppose you're right.'

'Where did Miss Buckley find the book?' I ask, leading the conversation in a different direction.

'In Sterling's room,' says Martha.

'Is there any other reason the girl might have wanted access to your daughter's things?'

'I can't think of any,' she says, 'although she was up there longer than I expected.'

'Was there anything she might have wanted other than a textbook?' Martha takes a moment to consider the question.

'I don't know. After she left I had the feeling something was either missing or out of place. I can't be certain.'

'Do you have trust issues with Miss Buckley?'

'I really don't know how to answer that.

I've just never taken to the girl.'

'May we have access to your daughter's room for an hour or so?'

'Yes, of course,' says Martha.

'Later today?'

'Yes, if you think it will help.'

'Can you think of anyone, anyone at all, who might have wanted to harm your daughter?' says Frack.

'No, I can't. She got along with everybody. She always said strangers were friends she hadn't met yet,' says Martha. 'You remember that, don't you Russ?'

'Yes Martha, she always said that.'

'Was she dating anyone?' I ask.

'Not since Carl Hammond. We were disappointed when they broke up, weren't we Martha?'

'Yes, it was puzzling. She couldn't have dated a nicer boy. Girls never stop talking when they're smitten and she hasn't mentioned a single boy's name since they split up.'

'Do you know the reason for the split?'

'She would simply shrug and say she was ready for a change.'

'So it was her idea?'

'It was.'

'How did he take it?' I ask.

'Like a gentleman as far as I know,' says Martha.

'When did they break up?'

'Sometime back in the summer. It's been a few months.'

'Have her habits or routines changed recently?'

'She's never been truant before, if that's what you mean,' says Russ. 'We bought her a car this summer, so some things were bound to change.' He sits up straighter in his chair. 'The car. You haven't mentioned the car.'

'It's been behind the hardware store since sometime Friday night,' says Frack. 'When it was still there today Gayle Shipley called us. I believe Sterling parked it with the expectation of returning before the buggies came to town. There was no sign of a struggle and the keys were under the mat. It's our opinion that she left on Friday night with someone she knew.'

'Someone with a car,' says Russ.

'That's our theory since she was found

several miles from town,' I say. 'The print team should be finished with it by now. You can pick the key up at the hardware store.'

'After I take Martha home, I'll come back with Harvey and get it, but first we want to see our daughter.'

I hand him one of Paula's cards from my wallet. 'The medical examiner will need a positive identification. I'll call ahead and let her know you're coming. If you think of anything that can help with the case, please call me or Officer Tilsley. We're available any time day or night.'

'I just remembered something,' says Martha, thumbing through her purse. 'I don't know how it slipped my mind.' She turns to Russ. 'Remember that rusty white van that kept parking at the bottom of our driveway? I took down the license number in my day planner.'

'What van?' says Frack.

'Just a white van with some strange man in it. He'd park and look up at the house for the longest time. If we went to the mailbox he'd drive off. Here it is,' she says, ripping the page out of a wallet-size calendar book. 'I was going to call the sheriff, but a week ago or so, he stopped coming by.'

I look at it and fold it into my notebook. 'We'll look into it,' I say. 'Did you get a description of the driver?'

'I'd say mid-thirtyish with dark hair and a mustache.'

'Did he ever get out of the van or try to engage you in conversation?'

'No, he just sat and watched. I asked Sterling if she knew him and she said she'd never seen him before.'

'Deputy Danner?'

'Yes, Mr. Seabright.'

'You didn't tell us how our daughter died. You just said that she'd been murdered.'

'She was strangled, sir,' I say.

'Was she . . . was she?'

'No. There were no signs of sexual assault. I want you to know that your daughter put up a very brave fight.'

Russ bursts into tears and Martha puts an arm around his shoulders.

* * *

After I finish throwing up in the garbage can behind the administration building, Frack and I sit in the patrol car in front of the school.

'I'm sorry. That wasn't very professional,' I say.

'It doesn't matter.'

He hands me his handkerchief and I wipe my eyes.

I take a couple deep breaths and blow them out. 'I was okay until . . . '

'You don't have to explain. It's hard dealing with other people's grief.' He looks at his watch. 'You're hungry. Come on, I'll feed you.'

'I have beer in my fridge. Let's get take-out from the Blue Bird and go to my place. I'll check on the dog. Then we need to question Madison Buckley and run the plate on the white van.'

Fargo must have heard the car pull in because he's waiting by the back door thumping his tail. I look around the apartment to make sure he hasn't ripped up the joint. I find everything is in order. This relationship might work out after all; if, of course, I get to keep him. I brush my teeth, gargle with mouthwash and fix my eyeliner. I grab a few beers from the fridge and head out the door.

'Come on, boy,' I say.

With his big head and wide paws Fargo is not that good with stairs, but we make it down without a catastrophe and walk to the picnic table by the river. I unwrap a burger and toss Fargo a high fly. He catches it mid-flight and swallows it whole. He can get all four feet off the ground when he's highly motivated.

'You're supposed to chew,' I scold. He puts his chin on my knee, looks up at me and twitches his eyebrows expressively. I put the hamburger wrapper on the ground and pour out the fries. I finish my hamburger, turn my face to the sun and close my eyes. One thing I like about Frack is how we can sit quietly without having to fill every moment with chatter. The beer loosens the knots in my stomach and I start to shake off the stress of the Seabright interview.

'He ate the paper,' says Frack.

I open one eye. 'What?'

'Fargo ate the wrapper when he inhaled

the French fries.'

'Oh, Fargo,' I say, snapping to attention. 'What were you thinking?'

Frack laughs. 'He looks like he does more eating than thinking.' Frack polishes off his second hamburger and puts the wrapper in the bag. 'You didn't ask the Seabrights if they're missing a dog.'

'They'd have said something. Besides, my brain was full of other things.' I gather up our papers and cans and carry them to the trash can behind the stairs. When I return Fargo is sleeping on top of the picnic table, his tongue hanging out to the side.

'Now what?' I say.

'Let him sleep. Believe me, this dog isn't going anywhere.' Frack pulls me against him. 'Look me in the eye.'

'What?' I say.

'You feeling better?'

I nod my head. 'You won't tell Mike I cracked will you?'

'You didn't crack,' he says. 'You were hungry. You'll be fine now.'

9

I stop tapping the computer keyboard and look over at Frack. 'The man who owns the van is Tyson Wetzel, age thirty-two. He has an extensive rap sheet of petty crimes starting when he was fifteen. He launched a career in shoplifting, then graduated to drug convictions and DWIs.'

'How about offenses against women?'

'There's nothing on record.'

'Any convictions for violent behavior?'

'Not one.'

'What's his address?'

'Twenty-two Railroad Spur.'

'That's the Alcola.'

The Alcola Arms, known locally as the Alcohol Hotel, is a three story brick building that sits in the middle of a field midway between Abundance and Ogdensburg. It sits beside an abandoned narrow-gauge railroad track that once serviced the now-defunct meat packing house. It's a dead end, both literally and figuratively, inhabited by penniless pensioners, addicts and ne'er-do-wells stuck in life's rapidly descending elevator.

As we get out of the car I see torn shades, cracked windowpanes and a few swamp coolers perched over crumbling sills. In the last eighteen months, six men have died here, two of natural causes, two from drug overdoses, one from suicide and one undetermined. A small group of men sit in the weeds along the tracks, smoking and eyeing us suspiciously as we pass through the double doors of the recessed entryway.

'Room 207,' I say, as Frack and I head up the staircase.

'This building has a bad case of halitosis,' says Frack.

'That's why we're not taking the elevator. Strange things go on in there.'

The man who opens to our knock matches the description given by Martha Seabright. Beneath his mustache his lips have a vague cyanotic tinge. He's wearing pajama bottoms and a wife beater. A self-fulfilling prophecy is inked on bulging biceps: Born To Lose. Lovely, just lovely.

'Mr. Wetzel?' says Frack.

'Who wants to know?'

'I'll give you a clue. I'm not the Good Humor man.'

I look past him into the cramped room. A sagging bed takes up most of the floor space. Slumped against the headboard is a woman of indeterminate age. Her hair is grey and matted and although she's three sheets to the wind, she manages to juggle a cigarette and a highball glass in one hand.

'I'm Deputy Tilsley and this is Deputy Danner,' says Frack.

'I paid the traffic ticket two days ago,' says Wetzel, leaning against the door-frame. 'It just hasn't updated to your computer yet.'

'This is in regard to another matter,' I say. 'May we come in?'

'My mother isn't ready to face the day yet.' He steps into the hall and closes the door behind him, an unlit cigarette clamped between his teeth. His eyes run up and down my uniform in a sexist, rather than sexual way. His message is clear even before he opens his mouth. He doesn't have to cooperate with a woman who has the audacity to think she's a real cop. He scrapes a kitchen match to life with his thumbnail and lights his cigarette. Of course, I'm hugely impressed. He leans into me with an exhalation of dragon breath. 'I'll give you thirty seconds, then I need to get back before my beer goes flat.'

Frack shoulder-slams him against the wall and sends a vibration echoing through the bones of the old building. I'm as shocked as Wetzel, who seems to have shrunken a few inches by the time Frack backs off. His cigarette falls to the floor. When he bends over to pick it up, I smile nicely and cover it with the toe of my shoe.

'Would you like to start over?' says Frack.

'Sure. What the hell. I guess I woke up on the wrong side of the bed.'

'I guess you did. I'm Deputy Frank Tilsley. This is Deputy Robely Danner, lead investigator. Some night when a jealous husband has your balls in a vise, she may take a bullet saving your worthless ass, so let's have a little respect here, okay?'

'Got it. Just tell me what you want.'

'We're responding to the report of a suspicious vehicle on Cloverdale Cut,' I say. 'The license plate corresponds with the one on your van. Would you care to comment on that?'

'The last time I checked, Cloverdale Cut is a public road.'

'That's true, but only five families live on it and you're not one of them,' I say. 'You can understand why your presence makes the home owners jittery. What's your business on that street?'

'I haven't been out there for a week.'

'Why did you stop going out there?' I ask.

'First you're on my case for being there. Now I'm suspect for *not* being there. I'm not aware that I've broken any laws.'

'You haven't answered my question, Mr. Wetzel.'

'Was there a question? I don't remember.'

‘What’s your business on Cloverdale Cut? Do you have a legitimate reason for parking at the bottom of the Seabrights’ driveway?’

‘So that’s what this is about, the lovely Miss Seabright. I don’t recall her having a problem with me when she was stranded on the highway in the middle of the night.’

‘When was that?’ asks Frack.

‘I don’t remember exactly. A couple weeks back I guess.’

‘Tell me about it.’

‘There’s not a lot to tell. I was coming home from the Fire Pit in Ogdensburg, when I saw this girl walking along the highway near the lake. It was dark. It was cold. I stopped and asked if she needed a lift. She said her car quit on her and her phone was dead so she couldn’t call for a tow. She got in the van. We drove back and I looked at the car. The gas gauge was on empty.’

‘Then what?’

‘I could have siphoned some fumes out of the van but I played dumb. She looked like a Nordic goddess and I wanted to get to know her. She called for a tow on my cell, but they were backed up and couldn't come out for a couple hours. She gave them her address and insurance information and told them to tow it to her house. Then I drove her home.'

'I'm glad chivalry isn't dead, Mr. Wetzel. I'd hate to see her taken advantage of by some shameless schemer,' I say. The sarcasm floats over his head like a soft summer cloud. 'Who was at the house when you dropped her off?'

'I don't know. All the lights were off except the porch light. I said, '*Aren't you going to invite me in for a nightcap?*' She said, '*I'm sorry but that's not possible.*' She got out, walked through the gate, closed it and left me sitting in the road like a bag of trash. No drink, not even a gratuity, and her living like a queen in a big fancy house.'

'I bet that made you hot under the collar,' says Frack.

'Yeah, I was pissed. Who wouldn't be?' The memory turns his ears red.

'What time was that?'

'Around midnight. I left The Pit earlier

than usual.' He pats an invisible pocket for cigarettes. Now that he's cooperating, Frack taps a Camel from his pack and lights it for him.

'Thanks,' he says. 'I can't think without a smoke in my hands.'

'Did she mention where she was coming from when she ran out of gas?' I ask.

'She had an argument with her boyfriend. I asked her what about? She said he wouldn't commit.' Wetzel finds that hilarious.

'Wouldn't commit to what?'

'Monogamy? Marriage? Who knows?'

'Did she mention her boyfriend's name?'

'If she did I wasn't paying attention.'

'So, why did you keep going back to Cloverdale Cut once you knew she didn't want you around?'

'I don't know. When I drink I do stupid things. If she had just said *thank you*, instead of making me feel like a bum, it would have made all the difference.'

'Where were you last Friday night and the early hours of Saturday morning?' asks Frack.

'That's easy. Friday was my birthday. You can check. I was celebrating at the Fire Pit, but ended up spending the night in the drunk tank. I don't remember getting hauled in, but that's where I was when the sun came up.'

'We *will* check your alibi, so I hope you're being truthful with us,' I say.

'Alibi? Why do I need an alibi?'

'That was the night Miss Seabright was strangled and her body left in the woods.'

Wetzel clutches his chest and stumbles against the door, his bones turned to rubber, his skin the color of clay.

'It's his heart,' I say. I grab his elbow. 'Easy, I've got you. Take a deep breath. Frack, call 911.'

'No ambulance,' say Wetzel. 'It's just a little valve problem I was born with. That's why I'm on disability. I'm not supposed to get upset.' Over the next couple minutes the color returns to his face. 'Geezus, you sure blindsided me with that one.'

'Are you sure you're alright?' I say.

'I'm sure. It comes and goes like that sometimes.'

'You swear you were nowhere near Sterling Seabright the night she was murdered?' says Frack.

'That's right. I wasn't out to kill her. I just wanted to . . . you know . . . get to know her.'

'Did you ever ask Miss Seabright how old she was?' asks Frack.

'No. I figured twenty-one, maybe twenty-two.'

'She was seventeen. A school girl. You'd better be more careful in the future.'

'I never would have guessed. I mean, tell me she didn't look twenty.'

'She did. That's why you have to be more careful. If you remember anything that might help us with this case, please give us a call.' Frack hands him a card.

'We're lucky he didn't drop dead on us,' I say, as we walk to the car. 'And no more rough stuff. If I can't survive someone's bad attitude I've got no business being a cop. Frack? Are you listening? Frack! Are you ignoring me?'

He looks at his watch. 'We'll have to step on it if we're going to catch the Buckley girl at school.'

10

We find Madison lying in a fetal position on a cot in the nurse's office. Scratches on her face mirror the ones we saw on our victim. Those girls really went at it. When I look at her frightened but defiant eyes, I know she's been expecting us.

'She's under the weather today,' says the school nurse. 'Her mother was supposed to be here two hours ago. If you'll excuse me I have to tend to a student with a sprained ankle.'

'We'll keep her company while she waits,' I say.

Madison rolls onto her back and covers her eyes with an arm.

'Does the light bother you?' I ask.

'Yes.'

'Let me turn off the overhead,' I say, flicking the switch. 'There. That's better. I'm Robely and this is Frank.'

She slowly sits up and looks at us. 'I know who you are.'

'I'm sorry you're not feeling well. Are you up to answering a few questions?'

'Not really,' she says.

'If you like, we can drive you home and we can talk on the way.'

'Mom will be here any minute. It would confuse things.'

'How about we come out to your house this evening?'

'What do you want to know?'

She sits on the edge of the bed and Frack brings her a paper cup of water from the sink. She drinks it in one breath. If you look beyond the scratches and the shabby clothes, she's a pretty girl, small and kittenish.

'You don't have to be afraid of us,' says Frack. 'Those scratches on your face must have been terribly painful.'

'A dog knocked me into a sticker bush,' she says.

'We're here to talk about your friend Sterling Seabright. You must be aware that she hasn't been in school.'

'I heard that.'

'Do you know why she's not in class?'

'I don't.'

'Do you know where she goes when she skips school?'

She turns to me with a frightened look in her eyes. 'I really don't.'

'Someone said that she was staying with you at the farm.'

'I don't know where they got that idea.'

'From what I gather, Mr. and Mrs. Seabright got that idea from you. They said you were out to their place on Saturday afternoon to pick up a textbook.'

'That's right. I remember now. We were studying for a test.'

'Then you did know where she was that day.'

'Well, maybe for a few hours, but I didn't know where she'd been before that and I don't know where she is now.'

'Did you pick up anything else while you were in Sterling's room?'

'I don't know what you mean.'

'Madison, I know you'd like to help us, but you're not making sense. Maybe it's because you're not feeling well, or maybe it's because you're not telling us the truth. Whether you help us or not we're going to get to the bottom of this.'

'Do you think I'm lying to you?'

'I think you're scared. That's what people do when they have something to hide.'

'But, I'm telling you the truth.'

'There's something you need to know. It's not good news, but if you don't hear it from us, you're going to hear it from someone else very soon. When you went out to the Seabrights' place on Saturday, Sterling had already been dead for several hours. A couple of young boys found her body. She had been strangled and left in the woods.'

Madison's jaw drops. She tries to say something but nothing comes out.

'I'm getting the nurse,' I say.

'What the hell is going on here?' A woman in a moth-eaten winter coat is standing in the doorway. She's wearing a 1950s hat with a green velvet rose pinned to the crown. 'What have you done to my child?'

'Mrs. Buckley?' I say.

'That's right.'

'She'll be fine,' says Frack. 'She's just

received some bad news.'

'Mom,' says Madison, her voice shaking. 'I want to go home.'

Mrs. Buckley points a long bony finger an inch from my nose and for a moment I'm looking at the witch from *The Wizard of Oz*.

'Stay away from us,' says Mrs. Buckley. 'I'm calling my lawyer as soon as I get home.'

I find her behavior astonishing.

'Why?' I say. 'Don't you want to know why we're here?

'Whatever it is, I'm sure it doesn't concern me or my family.' She grabs Madison by the arm with her talons and hustles her out the door. I'm speechless.

'That certainly went well,' says Frack.

* * *

We sit out front in the patrol car. Frack opens his window and lights a cigarette.

'Madison Buckley had no idea that Sterling Seabright was dead, but she certainly knew that something was wrong. Either that or she's a better actress than

Meryl Streep,' I say.

'I wonder what she's hiding, what she's so afraid of?'

'It could have to do with what she found in Sterling's room . . . or didn't. Drugs? Money? She may have an idea who murdered Sterling or where she went when she wasn't at school. I don't think we're going to get a lot out of her, especially with her mother calling the shots.'

'One thing's for sure. Those girls were in one hell of a cat fight, unless, of course, you believe they both fell into the same sticker bush,' says Frack.

'Let's check out Tyson Wetzel's alibi. He doesn't look like a guy who takes rejection in his stride.'

* * *

By the time Mavis Buckley pulls out of the parking lot, Madison is crying and trembling. Her mother waits until she's a block from school before flipping a stiff backhand into her daughter's face.

'What did you do that for?' says

Madison, covering her cheeks with her hands.

'Pull yourself together and tell me what the police want with you.'

'Mom, Sterling Seabright is dead!' Mavis Buckley gives her daughter an incredulous look. 'It's true. Someone killed her.'

'Who? How?' She looks at Madison, the car drifting and clipping the curb. She straightens out the steering wheel and steps on the gas.

'You came in before they had a chance to say. If you didn't want them focusing on us you shouldn't have made such a scene.'

'Don't lecture me. Why are they interested in you?'

'I don't know, Mom. I suppose they're talking to a lot of kids. I was her friend so my name was bound to come up. I don't know why you're so mad at *me*.'

'You know we can't have cops snooping around until that guy from Green Bay takes the crop off our hands. We've kept a low profile for all these months and we can't blow it now. One slip and we're ruined. I hope you didn't say anything incriminating.'

'Why would I do that?'

By 'the crop' Mavis means the two hundred marijuana plants air-drying in the shed. At the top of the real estate bubble the Buckleys took out a second mortgage on the farm. When the bubble burst they were underwater and the property could no longer support itself. Now they cultivate a more lucrative crop using hydroponics and halogen lights.

'If the cops want to see you again make sure it's not at the farm.'

'I have no control over that.'

'They've focused on you for a reason.'

'A parent can deny law enforcement access to a minor and they're not allowed to enter a closed gate without a warrant or an invitation.'

'Are you making that up?'

'It's common knowledge.'

'In that case keep your mouth shut. If we go down for this your dad and I are going to jail and you kids will be shipped off to foster care. Understood?'

'Mom, I didn't ask to be put in the middle of this. If we get busted it could ruin my chances for a scholarship.'

'Well, you *are* in the middle.'

11

Sterling Seabright's bedroom smells of talcum powder and perfume. Her paintings hang on the wall. Horses. Family pets. Trees. Rainbows. She loves make-up, fancy shoes and pretty dresses. On the shelf above the bed is a framed photo of Sterling and a handsome clean-cut boy riding a float. With their fair hair and blue eyes they could pass for sister and brother.

'That's got to be Carl,' I say.

'If she has a new love interest he hasn't knocked Hammond off the shelf,' says Frack.

'He looks like the all-American good guy.'

'So did Ted Bundy,' says Frack.

'Aren't you a little ray of sunshine.'

Frack and I pick through the room as carefully and thoroughly as cat burglars. In the chest are three large drawers of neatly stacked sweaters, polo shirts and jeans, the smaller drawers containing a colorful array socks and underthings, a portable hair dryer and a curling iron. On top of the mirrored dressing table are tubes of lipstick, bottles of perfume, boxes of powder and the usual feminine clutter. In the drawer are curlers, bobby pins, barrettes, pony tail cuffs and a manicure set. A box of tampons and a bottle of Midol tablets are shoved to the back corner. The receipt beneath the box puts the purchase date in mid-July. Neither the box nor the bottle has been opened.

I show the items to Frack. 'This strengthens Paula's theory of amenorrhea. Otherwise these would already have been opened and used.'

'She thought she was pregnant,' he says.

'That would be my guess.'

'Which means she was sexually active.

'They generally go hand in hand.'

'She must have been under a great deal of stress.'

'Her and somebody else?'

I pull a makeup bag from the same drawer. I unsnap it, looking for birth control pills. It contains a bracelet, tubes of lipstick and a compact of face powder. I check the contents of every purse on the closet shelf and the pockets of every coat. I find pennies, a movie stub and a broken earring. Frack looks inside the shoes and finds a five-dollar bill in the toe of an English riding boot. He sets it on the dressing table.

'She didn't seem to want for anything,' he says. 'I wonder where things went sideways?'

'Her options opened up when she got the car. That's when her secret life began.' I flip through the dresses on the rod, each hung from a padded satin hanger. 'Look at this,' I say, examining a see-through plastic garment bag containing a lavender semi-formal. 'The chiffon is stuck in the zipper. And look here. There's a square impression in the plastic at the bottom of the bag. Something was secreted in here. Let's run this by Mrs. Seabright.'

Martha Seabright has changed into grey slacks and a white sweater, her eyes red-rimmed, her demeanor composed. Like most Midwesterners there will be no histrionics. Any serious tears will be shed in private.

'What do you make of this?' I ask, showing her the zipper-snagged gown.

'Sterling would never have been that careless. She was saving that gown for the Christmas dance.'

'Do you know why someone would rifle through her things?'

'I have no idea, none whatsoever.'

'Money? Drugs? Jewelry?'

'She was an athlete. She'd never be involved with drugs and she carried her money with her. Did you find her purse?'

'See the impression in the plastic at the bottom of the garment bag? Something had been stored here. It's been removed and the bag carelessly zipped back up. Any idea what it might have been?'

'I can't imagine.'

'Maybe it's something she didn't want you or her father to know about. What about birth control pills?'

'Heavens no! She was still a child. Her life was an open book.'

Frack and I know better.

Car tires crunch over the acorns in the driveway and Martha looks out the window.

'That will be Russ and Harvey coming with the car,' she says. 'I'm sure they're starved about now. Would you care to join us for a little something?'

'I'm sorry, we can't. We still have a lot of ground to cover before the end of the day. Just one more thing. Do you have a key to the jewelry box? It's the only place we haven't looked.'

'She keeps it right here,' she says, lifting a teddy bear from the pillow and removing a key from a slit in the back seam. She unlocks the pink box. When she lifts the lid a tiny ballerina spins to 'Happy Days Are Here Again'. Martha chokes back tears. Inside the box is a string of pearls and a pair of diamond stud earrings. No money. No drugs. No birth control pills.

Frack had been standing quietly off to the side.

'What about a diary, Mrs. Seabright?' he asks. 'Did your daughter keep a diary?'

'Not that I'm aware of.' Her eyes scan

the dressing table. 'I knew something wasn't right. The Lalique perfume bottle is missing. I found it in an antique shop and gave it to Sterling on her last birthday.' She picks up a silver hair brush and presses it to her cheek.

'Other than you and your husband, who else enters this room?' I ask.

'Our housekeeper and Madison Buckley.'

'How long have you had the same housekeeper?'

'Fifteen years. Gertrude is of unimpeachable character.'

* * *

It's dark when we get back to the station. I type a report on the Wetzel and Buckley interviews while Frack connects with the jail. He walks up to my desk with his notes.

'At approximately 2:15 a.m. on the night of the homicide, Wetzel was scraped off the parking lot at Fire Pit. He was tossed in the drunk tank at 2:58 a.m. and released Saturday morning at ten.'

'Hmm,' I say. 'What time did he arrive at the bar?'

'The arresting officer didn't ask. It wasn't relevant because the body wasn't discovered until the next day. I'll call over to The Pit and see what they have to say.'

Twenty minutes later I finish up and swivel my chair toward Frack's desk.

'Any luck?' I ask.

'Marion Dubonnet was behind the bar that night. The place was Wetzel's home away from home and she'd baked him a birthday cake. She said he arrived late, about 12:30.'

'What state was he in?'

'Somewhere between buzzed and blitzed. When he left he was so plastered he couldn't make it to his car.'

'There's a big hole in his alibi. We need to know where he was before he arrived.'

* * *

Due to the heavy patient load the doctors at the clinic are backed up and several people decide to reschedule rather than wait. Carl is about to do the same when

Dr. Magnus asks him to stay. The longer he waits the more his imagination kicks in. What if he has cancer? What if he loses his testicles? What if he has an STD? His parents would go ballistic. That would mean he got it from Sterling and she got it from somewhere else. By the time he's called to the exam room he's in a state of high anxiety.

As it turns out, it's nothing half so dramatic. He almost faints with relief. It's a condition called varicocele, something he's never even heard of. It's a condition where veins that drain the testicle become inflamed. It prevents normal cooling of the tissue and leads to reduced sperm count. It's treatable. It's curable. He breathes a great sigh of relief.

'Some patients have no symptoms at all, for others like yourself it can become painful,' says Dr. Magnus.

'What are the implications? I mean, how will this affect my life?'

'Your sperm are lazy swimmers. Picture goldfish that go belly up in the bowl. As things stand today, the chance of your sperm fertilizing an ovum are zero to zilch, but that's something we're going to work on. It doesn't, however, mean you have permission to go hog wild with the girls. There are things a lot more worrisome than varicocele out there and some of them have become highly resistant to antibiotics. We'll discuss treatment at your next appointment with your parents present. Here's a prescription for the swelling and pain. Now, go home and be a good boy. You're going to be fine.'

'How about gym?'

'I want you in the library until further notice. You're to play no sports until we see how treatment goes. No cycling. No restrictive clothing.'

'Thanks, Doc. I got it.'

Carl is so relieved that the implications of what the doctor told him don't register until he's sitting in a fast food restaurant down the street from the clinic. It hits him between the eyes like a bowling ball. If Sterling is pregnant, he's not the one responsible. He's not Mr. Fifty Percent. He's become Mr. Zero, making someone else Mr. One Hundred Percent.

He pulls his cell phone from the backpack and dials Sterling's number . . . again. There's a nothingness on the other end. A vacuum. A void. At first he thought she was being stubbornly uncommunicative, as only she can be. Now, he has a haunting vision of her body lying motionless in an empty field, the phone at the bottom of the Little Papoose River. He should be relieved that Sterling Seabright is no longer his problem. Instead, he's filled with increasing dread.

* * *

It's dark when we arrive at Carl Hammond's house. The family lives in a well-maintained Arts and Crafts bungalow with a new coat of dusty olive paint and black shutters. There's a garden cottage in the back and a basketball hoop above the garage door. We park at the curb and climb the steps to the porch. A crystal hummingbird hangs in the front window. We knock on the door. We hear the gong of a grandfather clock and the yapping of a small dog. We knock again.

There's no car in the driveway and no lights on inside.

'No one's home,' I say.

'Tomorrow,' says Frack. 'First thing.'

We take the patrol car back to the station, but before I have a chance to get into my pickup, Frack jingles his keys at me.

'I'm driving you home,' he says. 'I'll pick you up for work in the morning.'

'Why?'

'I know about a vacant rental, four-fifty a month, utilities included.'

'Why so cheap?'

He opens the car door and I hop in. 'Because the owners are friends and I extolled the benefits of having a cop around the place.' As we drive toward Gladys's he lays it out for me. 'It's on the second level. Six hundred square feet of open space with a bath, a small kitchen area and a good furnace.'

'What about Fargo?

'He's welcome if he doesn't eat the woodwork.'

'I don't know if I want to be upstairs from people. I don't like to engage in conversation every time I pass through the house, people baking me cookies and telling me their problems. I get enough of that at the bar.'

'What if I told you the loft is above a horse stable, insulated, nicely finished off, the horse sold when their son went off to college.'

I snap to attention. 'I'll take it!'

He laughs. 'You look like you've been jabbed with a cattle prod. You haven't seen it yet.'

I give him a big kiss on the cheek. 'I don't have to. I've already moved in.'

'Okay,' he laughs, 'I'll show it to you in the morning.'

We pull up behind the bar. Fargo jumps down from the picnic table, stretches and yawns. He's already starting up the stairs when we get out of the truck.

'I want to walk you up,' says Frack.

'Why?'

'A gentleman always sees a lady to her door.'

'You're making me nervous,' I say.

'You're extremely intuitive.'

We climb the stairs. I let the dog inside. Frack and I stand on the landing outside the door.

'Alright, what's on your mind?' I ask.

He looks at me with those lethal blue-green eyes and a half-smile on his face.

'What?' I say.

'You know it's inevitable, don't you Robely?'

'Solving the case you mean?'

'No, not solving the case. You've been alone for three years. Sooner or later you're going to fall for someone and I want it to be me.'

'I can't believe you said that. Assuming I did, or that I already have, how do you know it isn't because you're so much like . . . like . . . you know who?'

'Good old David? I find that encouraging. It proves I'm your type of guy. I already know you're my kind of woman. I can feel it.'

'And I know where.'

We both suppress a smile.

'You're a stunner Robely, kind, smart and brave under fire. I want so badly . . .

so desperately to . . . get . . . you . . . in . . . bed. There, I've said it,' he announces, his arms outstretched, palms up in a supplicating gesture.

I burst out laughing. 'Why don't you tell me what you really want?' Still smiling, I quietly rest my forehead against his chest.

'I can't. Not yet.'

'Because of David?' he says. I look into his eyes.

'Because of me, Frack. There are things I haven't told you about his death. Things I've never told anyone. When I do, you might not think I'm so special.'

'Like what?'

'Another time.'

'Promise?' he says.

'When the time is right.'

He puts a finger beneath my chin and turns my face up to his. He kisses me very softly which feels very good. I put a hand on his lower back and pull him against me. I feel his hard stomach against mine and his body heat through my clothes. He pulls my shirt out at the waist, his hands against my bare skin. I imagine what it would be like with Frack and I don't want him to stop. As the flag of surrender is about to shoot up the pole, I gently untangle myself from his embrace. I touch his cheek.

'I think I hear my mother calling,' I say. I step inside and close the door.

* * *

Sometime in the night I wake to a noise and I'm suddenly a child again, with a child's fear of the dark. In that brief moment before I'm fully awake, I'm seven again, or nine, or thirteen, Gladys passed out in her room, her latest one-night stand walking the hall and stealing quietly into my room.

I'd run to Gladys and shake her awake and a wall would go up between us. She'd accuse me of having an overactive imagination, of wanting to be the center of attention. Jake or Ralph or Calhoun would never do such a thing unless they were provoked. She told me to shut up about it, or the authorities would put me in juvie or a psychiatric ward. Nice little girls don't know about such things.

I became an angry, distrustful child who slept with a hatpin under her pillow and a chair beneath the doorknob. My teachers noticed the change, had their suspicions, but a small town quickly divides into warring factions and speaking up was a risky proposition. Instead, they avoided eye contact and sat me at the back of the room so they could pretend I didn't exist. I became *that child* with all the implications that went with it.

Fargo raises his head from the pillow and growls deep in his throat. The doorknob rattles. I take my gun from the nightstand. I hear heavy breathing and see a shadow in the crack beneath the door. I pull back the hammer. The click is loud and metallic in the silence.

'Sorry,' says a male voice. 'I thought this was the bathroom.' A floorboard creaks and footsteps retreat down the hall.

I've stayed above the bar all of these years, not because I want to be here, but because I'm afraid for Gladys and her careless lifestyle, of the men who bring their shadowy credentials and illusive pasts into her life and between her sheets. What I can't do is protect my mother from herself. I'm twenty-seven. Tomorrow I cut the cord.

12

Frack introduces me to the Macumbers. I love the property the moment I see it. There's a big white farmhouse, a grape arbor to the left of the veranda, a red barn and large stable. Jim and Jane Macumber are an upbeat, down to earth, middle-aged couple.

'This is it,' says Jim, giving me the guided tour of the loft. 'It's warm in winter and tolerable in summer, but if you're looking for marble countertops and stainless steel appliances, you're barking up the wrong tree.'

The loft is everything I'd hoped for. I expected the stairs to be as steep as a firehouse pole, but to my surprise they're shallow and broad, a real staircase instead of a ladder. There's genuine wood paneling, the sweet smell of hay, a front window overlooking the barnyard and a back window opening onto the creek between the stable and the windbreak.

'I love it Mr. Macumber. When can I move in?'

'Any time you're ready, provided you call us Jim and Jane and don't let the dog eat the geese.'

I write him a check for first, last and security deposit. 'I'm moving in tonight,' I say.

Frack and I hop in his truck and head for the station, already focused on the case.

* * *

Madison wakes up with a headache and Mavis lets her stay home from school. She's still expected to gather eggs before she's allowed to go to the loft where it's peaceful and private. Mavis notices her daughter's loss of weight, how she keeps to herself and speaks only when spoken to. Everyone is hungry, but when Mavis mentions food stamps or public assistance her husband Levi slams his fist on the table and turns purple with rage.

'I'd rather starve than take welfare,' he says. 'They might take the farm, but they're not taking my dignity.'

'What about the rest of us? Madison has to go to school looking like Little Orphan Annie while all the other kids have new clothes and Toby's grades are dropping because all he can think about is food. The kids are still growing for god's sake.'

'Be patient, Mavis. One more week and we'll all be eating like King Henry the Eighth.'

Madison picks up the perfume bottle and blows away a few bits of hay. The clear glass has an allusive violet hue, the stopper fluted like the graceful wings of a bird. She dabs a little scent behind her ears and cries when it brings back memories of splashing in the Blue Hole and looking up at a sky of dizzying stars at The Dells. Those days are never coming back and neither is Sterling. It's hard to keep hating a dead girl, even if she did steal Eddie. You have to revisit your grievances over and over to keep them alive and it's more exhausting with each effort. She picks up the diary and continues where she left off.

It's just a matter of convincing Mr. Gregory that I can hold my own with the boys. I'm as good as anyone on that team, better than some, not quite as good as Carl, but no one else is either. I'm told Gregory is very close to caving in. Another talk or two with Coach Breyer and he'll be on board. It would be such a conquest, such a validation of my athletic skills. I mean, take a look at me. I'm fast and strong. I'm a lean, mean machine.

The boys would never accept a girl on their team no matter how good she was. They'd bloody her nose, sort of *accidentally on purpose*, or monopolize the ball so she couldn't demonstrate her skill. It might not be fair, but that's the way it is.

I see as much as I can of E. If I continue hanging out with Madison and Carl, they'll figure things out. Well, maybe not Carl; he's too trusting for his own good. But, Madison is sharp.

As if she hasn't already guessed that Sterling stole Eddie, gorgeous Eddie with his soulful eyes and dramatic bearing. They used to read poetry together, Ginsberg and Housman. They talked about art and music and civil rights. They were soulmates until Sterling came along and ruined it all.

'I hate her!' she whispers, slamming the diary shut. But, even as she says it, she knows it's not true. She pulls the phone from the pocket of her overalls. There's only ten minutes left on it. She tries Carl's number for the third time in an hour and gets no answer.

* * *

A print-out of Carl's class schedule leads Frack and me to the gym. I look at the players on the court, but don't see the blond boy who rode the float with Sterling Seabright. The coach stops practice and trots over to us, his auburn curls tumbling over the forehead of a handsome round face.

'We're looking for Carl Hammond,' says Frack.

'Oh yes, the Hammond boy. He's not here. Is there anything I can help you with?'

'Do you know where we can find him?'

'He's assigned to the library this morning. Just follow the sidewalk past the quad and you'll bump right into it.'

'Thank you,' says Frack.

We find Carl restacking National Geographic videos at the back of the room. He's clean-cut and conservatively dressed in a blue shirt with a button-down collar and pressed khakis. The librarian suggests we use her private office and we settle around a long table spread with newly arrived books.

'Do you know why we're here, Mr. Hammond?' I say.

'I have no idea. What's going on?'

'Mr. Hammond . . . '

'Everyone calls me Carl. Mr. Hammond is my dad.'

'Carl it is.'

'Has something happened to my parents?'

'No, I'm sure your parents are fine,' I say. 'Can you tell me where you were last Friday evening?'

'I was at home watching TV. Why?'

'Can someone verify that?'

'I was there when my parents left for a

dinner dance and I was sleeping when they got home.'

'So, you don't have an alibi for the *entire* evening.' He gives us a wary look.

'Why? Do I need one?' he asks, with a surprised look on his face.

'Are you acquainted with a girl named Sterling Seabright?' asks Frack.

'Yes. Why? Is she alright?'

'I heard you two were pretty close.'

'We dated last year. Do you know where she is?'

'Has she been missing?' asks Frack.

'She's been truant. I've been worried.'

'When is the last time you spoke with her?' I ask.

'A little over a week ago. I can't remember the exact date.'

'In person?'

'On the phone.

'Did you call her or did she call you?'

'She called me,' he says. 'What difference does it make? What's going on?'

'What did you talk about?' I ask. He's annoyed. I don't blame him. A minefield of questions coming at him, while he's hung in the air like laundry on a line.

'She said she was sorry she broke up with me the way she did. Not that she regretted breaking up, just the way she did it.'

'And how was that?'

'She stopped taking my calls. She cut me off like I never existed.'

'That must have made you mad.'

'I wasn't mad. Well, maybe a little. I was confused. We hadn't argued. I thought things were fine between us.'

'When did this happen?'

'Sometime in July. No exact date. She just drifted, you know, like the fog *on little cat feet*.'

'You read Frost,' says Frack.

'Doesn't everyone?

'Was that the entire focus of your last conversation? To apologize for the way she left you?'

There's a brief but telling pause. I already know we're going to get a quickly edited response.

'That was it. It was a brief conversation. If you don't believe me, pull the phone records.'

'When is the last time you spoke with Madison Buckley?' I ask.

'A few days ago. She's been calling my cell this morning, but I've been in class.'

'Have you seen the scratches on Madison Buckley's face?'

'Everyone has. Why? Has Sterling pressed charges against her? Is that what this is about?'

'Do you know what sparked the altercation?' says Frack.

'Of course. I was there.'

'You were there?' says Frack. 'Where's there?'

'My friend Eddie Breyer's house on Stonebridge.' E.B. I'm thinking about the initials on the knife again. 'I'm the one who broke it up. Madison accused Sterling of stealing Eddie away from her.'

'Are you telling me that Eddie and Madison were an item?'

'At one time.'

'What day was the fight?'

'It was last Thursday evening.'

'But, you said you hadn't spoken with her for a week or more.'

'We *didn't* speak on Thursday night.

Eddie and I were playing chess. There was a knock and Eddie opened the door. It was Sterling. Madison followed her there. Sterling was jumped from behind and never made it inside. I pulled them apart and restrained Madison while Sterling raced to her car and took off.'

'Who got the worst of it?' says Frack. Carl's eyes cut sharply to his face.

'They *both* got the worst of it.'

'And all of this was over a boy named Eddie? He must be quite a guy.'

'Listen, boys are what girls fight about. Girls are what boys fight about. But, this time it was based on a misunderstanding. Sterling had nothing to do with the breakup. She and Eddie are just friends. They like to talk. They're into art.'

'How can you be so sure she didn't steal Eddie?'

He considers the question. 'I'm not going to answer that. Go talk to Eddie.' He runs fingers through his sunny crop of hair. 'Have the Seabrights filed a missing persons report on Sterling? I've been calling her cell for days, but she hasn't picked up.'

Frack and I look at one another. This is something we'd overlooked.

'What's her cell phone number?' I ask. He tells me and I write it down. 'You say Madison has been trying to reach you?'

'Yes, all morning. I'm going to call her back between classes.'

'She's calling with bad news, Carl.'

'What do you mean?' I see him brace for what's coming. He has that *please don't say it* look on his face, the one I've witnessed too many times in the past. Having to *say it* never gets easier.

'Sterling Seabright's body was found in the woods on Saturday.'

Carl looks like he's been socked in the stomach. 'You're not joking?'

'I'm not,' I say. 'I'm sorry.'

'What happened?'

'She'd been strangled.'

'Geezus!' He rubs his temples. 'Do you know who did it?'

'Not yet. How about you? Any ideas?'

Another pause. He shakes his head.

'You're sure?'

'How would I know something like that?'

'One more question,' says Frack. 'Were you and Miss Seabright intimate?'

'What do you mean?

'I think you know what I mean.'

'We're through here. I've answered enough questions.'

Back in the quad I turn to Frack. 'He knows more than he's telling.'

Frack laughs out loud. 'We're cops. Everyone knows more than they're telling. Try Sterling's cell.'

I punch in the number and listen to the silence. 'It's dead,' I say.

I call Martha Seabright and we talk briefly. When I'm off the phone I say, 'Sterling had the cell phone with her when she left on Wednesday. Her mother says she takes it everywhere, that it has a black glass front and a pink rubber case and if we find her purse, we'll find her phone.'

* * *

In the attendance office we learn that Eddie Breyer is absent so we head out to Stonebridge Court. Eddie lives in a two-story house of grey fieldstone in an upscale neighborhood backing onto a leafy ravine. When we knock, the door is opened by an older woman in a frilly white apron.

'I'm Deputy Danner and this is Deputy Tilsley,' I say. 'Are you Mrs. Breyer?'

'I'm Doris Stebbins,' she says. 'I keep house for the Breyers. Won't you come in?' We follow her into a large tiled foyer containing tropical plants in large ceramic urns. Through an archway is a living room filled with heavy Mediterranean furniture and wrought-iron chandeliers.

'Are Eddie's parents in?' I ask.

'His father is working and his mother passed away years ago.'

'We'd like to speak with Eddie if we could.'

'He's in his room, all broken up about the death of a friend. I'm sure everyone who knew her is shaken by the dreadful news.'

'We'll try not to upset him, but it's important we speak with him.'

'He won't even open his door so I can bring him a tray.'

'May we try? It'll save us making a second trip.'

'He's up the stairs, first door on the right. When his father is home Eddie can't be himself, so don't be surprised if you find him in his comfort clothes.'

What are comfort clothes? Sweats? Pajamas? I don't ask. We ascend a curved staircase and enter a broad hall. There's an Oriental runner over the Spanish tile and quality El Greco prints on the textured yellow walls. I knock softly on his door.

'Eddie, it's Deputies Danner and Tilsley. May we have a moment of your time?'

'Not now. I'm having a nervous breakdown,' he says, in a voice choked with sobs.

'We know you're upset, Eddie, and that's okay. We all are.'

I hear the bed squeak. A deadbolt slides in the track and he opens the door just wide enough to peek through the crack.

'Who's he again?' he asks, eyeing Frack suspiciously.

'My partner, Frank Tilsley. Believe me,

he's an okay guy.'

'Alright,' he says opening the door so we can enter. 'I just don't want to be ganged up on, you know, good cop, bad cop like on TV.'

'That's not going to happen,' says Frack. 'We just need to ask a few questions.'

Eddie Breyer is devastatingly handsome, tall and slender in his silk Japanese robe and monkey-fur boa. He has high dramatic cheekbones and a decidedly androgynous aspect, emphasized by smudged mascara tears beneath his eyes. A blade of straight dark hair sweeps the left side of his face. I avoid eye contact with Frack. I'm not in the mood for funny looks or eye-rolling.

Drapes of scarlet velvet hang from wrought-iron rods and a bed with a massive carved headboard anchors the house to the center of the earth. Eddie motions toward matching Spanish thrones upholstered in midnight-blue brocade. Frack sits, but I'm busy admiring the display of artwork on the walls and the dozens of canvases stacked along the baseboards. On the easel is the portrait of a beautiful blonde-haired girl beside a grey Arabian horse, both her hair and the horse's mane blowing in the wind.

'Sterling Seabright,' I say. 'You're an artist.'

'Yes.' He wipes a tear with the tip of his boa.

Eddie's paintings are executed in bold slashes of color with an eye for balance, perspective and outrageous individuality.

'You paint like the German expressionists,' I tell him.

A light goes on in his eyes. 'Not many people would know that. I love Kandinsky, Campendonk and Von Werefkin,' he says.

'Your art is amazing.'

'My father threatens to burn them. He wanted a sweaty jock for a son, not an *arteest*. That's the way he pronounces it: *arteest*. You can only imagine what a disappointment I am.'

I've struck a nerve. A raw one. 'I'm sorry to hear that. Not everyone has an eye for art.'

'He makes life as difficult as he possibly can.'

'In what way?'

'For one thing, the school bus doesn't come out this way and he won't let me drive his winter car even though it sits in the garage gathering dust. My ride didn't come this morning so I never made it to school. According to my father, I will have no privileges until I *straighten up and fly right*, his words imparting a dual meaning.'

'Mrs. Stebbins said you lost your mother years ago. That must have been very difficult.'

'Yes, Veronica Coronetti. She was a beautiful Italian heiress. She understood me. Dad's had a grand time living off what's left of her fortune.'

'How did she die?'

'She was found dead in the bathtub. Drowned. Try drowning yourself in the tub when you've got nothing better to do. It's nearly impossible.' He sits on the edge of the bed. 'Forget what I said. I'm having a bad day.'

'You lost a friend. You're entitled.'

'If it weren't for Mrs. Stebbins I'd hang myself in the stairwell. I think about it all the time,' he says, running long expressive fingers through his hair. 'Sterling and I were going to San Francisco to study art after graduation. Now I can't decide what to do.'

'Was she any good? Her art, I mean?' He pauses and sighs deeply before answering.

'Not so bad that she couldn't improve,' he says, with an apologetic smile. 'That's her portrait of me.' He points to a giant canvas above an overflowing bookcase. 'I look like a cross between Rudolf Nureyev and Lady Gaga.' He glances toward the ceiling. 'Sorry, Sterling my love. I cannot tell a lie.'

'How did you hear the bad news?' I ask, settling on throne number two.

'Madison left a message on my machine last night,' he says. 'She's still ticked off at me for splitting up with her, so I thought it was a cruel joke. Then Carl called a few minutes ago and confirmed it. I can't believe she was murdered. Everyone loved her. I mean, she was a princess.'

'Does that include Madison Buckley?'

'Madison was just venting her angst. She hated Sterling to the degree she loved her. That might be a hard concept to grasp, but that's the way it is.'

'She thinks Sterling alienated your affections, to use an antiquated term. Carl says that's what triggered the fight.'

'When I broke up with Madison I told her I wanted to play the field. Not the most sensitive choice of words. The problem was we weren't envisioning the same ballpark, if you catch my drift.'

'You're not into girls.'

'Oh, I *love* girls,' he says, tossing his forelock like a circus pony. 'They help me strike just the right note with my costumes and accessories. Of course, when I was with Madison I was still playing it straight, so I have to take responsibility for her hurt feelings. Now, I have one foot out of the closet and the other one on a banana peel. With Sterling gone, I don't know what I'll do after graduation. About my future that is.'

'Yes you do, Eddie. You pack your easel and go to San Francisco. You're going to explode onto the art scene like a hydrogen bomb. Don't let *anyone* talk you out of your dreams. The world is full of sweaty jocks, but it can never have too many *arteests*.'

He can't help smiling. 'It sounds so much nicer when you say it.'

'Did you see Sterling again after the cat fight?'

'No one did that I know of. She never came back to school. Generally, we'd chat every day on the phone, but I never heard from her again. If she called I was going to say, *Why didn't you call? I thought you were dead*. But, she really is dead.' A tear drops on his kimono and turns a pink flower petal red.

I take the jack knife out of my pocket.

'Have you ever seen this?' He takes it from my hand, looks at it closely, runs a finger over the initials.

'Is that E.B. or B. something else? They could be my initials, but I don't recognize it.'

'Are you sure?'

'Well, maybe not one hundred percent, but it doesn't ring a bell.' He hands it back to me.

'Thank you, Eddie.'

'Is it important?'

'We don't know yet.' I put it back in my pocket. 'Can you think of anyone who might have wanted to harm Sterling Seabright?'

'No one. Certainly no one from Abundance.'

'Not even Madison Buckley?'

He raises an eyebrow. 'I think she got it out of her system the other night. Besides, Carl said Sterling was strangled. Madison is tiny. It would be like a mouse strangling a giraffe.'

'Was Sterling seeing anyone romantically?'

'I don't know. I asked her, but that's one area of her life she wouldn't talk about. She wasn't into explaining herself. You've heard the expression, *never complain, never explain*. That was Sterling. I suspect she had her secrets, but who am I to talk?'

'Where were you last Friday evening?'

'Is that the night she was killed?'

'Yes.'

'Performing with the Shakespeare group in New London. The Harlequins. I'm billed as Edward Coronetti. That's also how I sign my art. After the show I went for pizza with friends at Cappolino's. Ask Lucca, the owner. He'll remember me.'

'What part did you play?' asks Frack, breaking his silence.

'Romeo, of course,' he says, hand over heart. 'Need you ask?'

'I bet every young man in the county auditioned for that part.'

'The competition was absolutely savage, but I died more convincingly than the others. I put my heart and soul into it.'

'Thank you for talking with us, Eddie,' I say. 'Listen, if you get to thinking about ropes and stairwells, please give me a call.' I hand him my card. 'Anytime, night or day.'

'I hope you find out who killed Sterling. When you do, he should be boiled in oil.'

'Keep your ear to the ground. Let me know if you hear anything interesting.'

On our way out, I show the knife to Mrs. Stebbins, but she can't recall having seen it either.

⋆ ⋆ ⋆

'Sterling Seabright isn't the only princess in Abundance,' says Frack, when we pull away from the curb.

'Come on Frack, everyone has a right to their place in the sun.'

'You melted right through his defenses.'

'He knows I like him.'

'You're a sucker for marginal personalities.'

'Oh really? Have you looked in the mirror lately?'

'Me? Ever think about the weird things people like that do in bed?'

'*Everybody* does weird things in bed. That's why we don't do them on street corners.'

Frack laughs and takes a long drag from his cigarette. He exhales lazily through his nose. 'I think we can take

Eddie off our suspect list, unless you think he strangled her with his boa.'

'He's also got an air-tight alibi. He was in front of an audience.'

'He *said* he was in front of an audience. What if he had a stand-in that night? I intend to check it out.'

'I think you should.'

We spend the rest of the afternoon interviewing Sterling's teachers, schoolmates and teammates. We check the contents of her locker and find nothing of a personal nature. Everyone we talked to described her as friendly, popular and competitive with a strong sense of entitlement. She talked freely about basketball, horse shows and art, but not about her love life. If she was seeing a guy, no one knew who he was. It was suggested he might be a boy from another town, a recent graduate or a college student.

Frack makes a few calls when we return to the station. 'Eddie Breyer's alibi checks out,' he says. 'He partied until 2:00 a.m. after his five curtain calls.' Frack slumps back in his chair. 'What if Gregory is right? What if it was random. A stranger. An outsider. A girl like that is bound to attract attention wherever she goes.'

'I don't think so. It's going to be a local, maybe someone we've already brushed shoulders with.'

'What's that, female intuition?'

'Is there any other kind?'

13

At the end of the day, Frack and I drive to the bar and load our pickups with the sum of my worldly possessions. I travel light: an antique bed with a scrolled iron headboard, a dresser, book case, clothes, kitchen items, books and a dog. By the time we're finished packing it's dark, the green neon sign in the window of the bar flickering and buzzing, cars filling up the parking lot out front.

We're about to shove off when Gladys comes running out of the exit door in black leather pants and a tight Harvey Davidson t-shirt. She has small silver skulls in her ears and a studded dog collar around her neck.

'I can't believe you're really doing this, sweetie,' she says. 'I thought you'd come to your senses.'

'I need to get out of here, Gladys. This move is long overdue.'

Frack is leaning casually against his

truck smoking a cigarette. Gladys gives him an accusatory look. He smiles and gives a helpless shrug.

'What about my thirty days' notice?' she says.

'Ever hear of constructive eviction?' I say. 'When you let strangers camp out in my room, you broke the lease.'

'Come on, honey. It was just Jackie and Howie. They're like family.'

'Your family. Not mine. I love you, mom, but I'm out of here.'

'What about my last month's rent? If you don't give notice, don't I get thirty days' rent?'

'There's an envelope in the freezer compartment of the fridge. If I don't get a receipt are you going to come back on me later for non-payment?'

'Oh, for heaven's sake,' she says. 'You think I'd cheat my own daughter?' I'm tempted to mention her two-foot-long rap sheet, but decide it's not the daughterly thing to do. I kiss her on the cheek, hand her the room key and climb into the truck. 'So, where are you moving to?'

'A quiet place in the country. I'll call

you when I get settled.'

I whistle Fargo into the cab and follow Frack out of the lot.

* * *

It's been a long day, almost eleven by the time we have the loft semi-organized. We've finished off a sixpack between us and collapse on top of the bed, happy and spent, our faces warm from exertion. I've dressed up the bed in new navy-blue sheets and the quilt I bought at the Amish craft store. Fargo is sleeping in front of the furnace, chasing rabbits in his sleep, his head resting beside the food bowl.

The open window above the bed lets in the rushing sound of the creek and the subtle, blended scents of autumn blowing in off the fields. There's a change in the air, the chill replaced by a balmy lightness. I'm about to say there's a hint of rain in the wind when the first drops hit the window like marbles spilling onto a glass coffee table.

'I'd say I don't know how to thank you

for your help, but I'm sure you'd have a smart answer.'

'I do,' he says, smiling. 'Want to hear it?'

'I'm wearing my favorite t-shirt,' I say.

'It's cute. Pink with little red hearts on the front.'

'There's nothing under it,' I whisper.

'I noticed. Why is that?'

'Why do you think?'

'I'm not into heavy thinking at the moment.' He rolls onto an elbow and gives me a questioning, somewhat apprizing look. 'You're not drunk are you?'

'Pleasantly buzzed is all.'

'Maybe a little *too* pleasantly. Aren't you afraid I'll take advantage of you?'

'Afraid isn't exactly what I'm feeling right now.'

'Can you walk a straight line, count backwards from one hundred?'

'I can't even do that when I'm sober. Lock me up for the night officer. I want to plead guilty'

'Guilty to what?'

'Help me with my shirt and I'll show you,' I say, raising my arms.

I blink and my shirt is draped over the lampshade, casting the room in a soft rosy glow. He buries his face in my hair, his hands gliding over my skin . . . working man's hands, strong and callused.

'My god, you're as soft as velvet,' he says.

I unbutton his jeans and he kicks them off.

'Why tonight?' he says. 'You've fought me off so long, why now?'

'I had to get away from the bar first. I need to make new memories.'

'I can help with that.'

Our lips come together and a whimper catches in my throat. There's a flash of lightning and thunder rolls across the sky. My jeans hit the side of the dresser, the change in my pocket rolling across the floor.

His elbows are on both sides of my head, his fingers in my hair, his weight suspended above me. Resisting him all these months has been like carrying the Rock of Gibraltar up Mount Everest. I give in. I let go. I'm free, a feather on the wind.

Afterward I lie against his side, quietly, deeply contented. It's been a long time since I've revealed my soft, submissive side. The cop life takes something out of you after a while, always being in charge and calling the shots, looking confident when you're shaking in your shoes. Tonight I'm back in touch with the woman under all that defensive armor.

After a long interlude of soft breathing and listening to the rain, Frack says, 'Tell me about David.'

'Right now?'

'I can't think of a better time. We need to get the elephant out of the room, don't you think?'

'It's a hard place to revisit. If I tell you the story I'm afraid you might not like me anymore.'

'You can't trust me unless you test me.'

'Oh boy. Alright, I'll try. It happened on a night like tonight, at least that's the way it ended. David was working at the lumber yard that Saturday. It was a nice autumn day and he'd ridden his motorcycle to work. I had a bad virus of some kind. I needed to get to the doctor, but my car was running roughly. It quit every time I stopped at an intersection. I found out a few days later that I'd gotten a tank of contaminated gasoline, but at the time I didn't know what the problem was. David said to leave it at his place and take his car, that he'd check mine out on Sunday.' I stop talking. 'I need a cigarette.'

'You don't smoke. Keep going.'

'He wanted me to spend the night at his place because it's hard to get any rest at the bar. The doctor gave me a prescription for antibiotics, but by the time I got out of his office it was dark and the drugstore was closed. I was too sick to drive another twenty miles to the all-night Walgreens, so I came back to the cabin and figured I'd wait until the following day to fill it. On David's way home that night it started to rain. He'd been home about thirty minutes when the storm came on full force. I thought the wind would take the roof right off the cabin. That's how bad it was.

'I took a double dose of Benedryl to knock me out, but I woke coughing sometime in the night with a 103-degree fever. David decided to drive to the Walmart for my antibiotics, but when he got to the garage . . . ' I cover my mouth with my hand.

'You're doing fine. What happened next?'

'You don't want to know.'

'I really do. You've said the words inside your head a million times. Now I want you to say them out loud. If you don't you're always going to be stuck back there instead of here with me.' He gives me an encouraging squeeze.

'I'd left the lights on in his car and the battery was dead, but I didn't know that until later. Everything that followed was my fault. I heard him roar off on the Harley in the worst of the storm. Down the highway a farmer thought he had the road to himself and decided to move his tractor from the field to the barn across the road. David also thought he had the road to himself. The night was pitch black. The tractor had no lights or reflectors. David drove into the back of it at fifty miles an hour, never even knew it was there. The coroner said he died instantly. It never would have happened if I didn't leave the lights on, if I hadn't run down his battery.'

Frack holds me for a long time as my tears soak into his t-shirt.

'You're going to be okay,' he says. 'Trust me on that. Now, I'd like to tell you a story,' he says, wiping away my last tear with his finger. 'Do you want to hear it?'

'Sure.'

'I had an older brother named Cal. He was a great guy and I wanted to be just like him. When I was in eighth grade and he was a senior, he walked into the woods and put a bullet in his head. He was captain of the football team. He had a girlfriend who adored him and a family he loved. His grades were good. He was healthy. There were no outward signs of depression.

'Everyone who was close to him . . . me . . . my mom . . . my dad . . . his best friends . . . we all searched our souls until each one of us convinced ourselves we were to blame for what happened, even though we couldn't say just why. That's what we do when we can't make sense of a tragic situation. We find reasons to blame ourselves, to attach some kind of logic to an unexplainable event. It took me years to work through that experience, but I finally did. It doesn't hold me captive anymore.

'My point is this. If you don't make peace with your loss, you can *if* yourself to death like you've been doing for three years. You can do it for the rest of your life and you still won't have any answers. If you didn't get bad gasoline. If you weren't sick. If there wasn't a storm. If the battery wasn't dead. If the farmer hadn't moved his tractor. If the tractor had tail lights. See what I mean? You loved him and he loved you. That's all you need to take away from this.'

* * *

My pager goes off. The loft is dark except for the luminous dial on the digital clock. It's 2:45. I stub my toe on the night stand and almost tip over the lamp trying to find my bearings in my new surroundings. On the fifth ring I find the light switch and grab my pager from the top of the bookcase. I look back at the bed. It's empty. Frack is gone.

'Deputy Danner here,' I say, shaking the cobwebs from my head.

'This is your 911 operator.'

'What's happened?'

'Gunfire has been reported on Lake Road. The first responders have been called but they can't gain access until law enforcement clears the scene. The shot came from inside the fifth cabin down from the bait shop.'

'One shot?'

'I believe so.'

'How many people are involved? Are we talking about an altercation or what?'

'A single gunshot. That's all the information I have.'

'I'm on my way. Please notify Officer Tilsley and have him meet me at the scene.'

14

I fly down the empty highway, drinking yesterday's cold coffee from my thermos. After ten minutes I pull onto Lake Road a mile from the town limits. The rain has slowed to a drizzle by the time I drive past the bait shop. Forty yards ahead a knot of people shiver beneath umbrellas outside a row of cabins.

After Labor Day the population at the lake drops off, leaving a handful of year-rounders. The fire truck and ambulance crew is parked to the side of the drive. I jump from the truck and walk up to Cappy Hendricks, the Fire Chief. He's a rugged, big-boned fellow who looks like he could carry Arnold Schwarzenegger from a burning building.

'Are you okay?' he asks. 'Your eyes are all swollen.'

'Allergies,' I tell him. 'Who lives in 5?'

'According to the neighbors, a senior citizen named Betsy Warren.'

‘And they’re sure the gunshot came from this cabin?’

‘*I’m* sure,’ interjects a man in an Indian blanket robe and a transparent bubble umbrella. ‘I was in the bathroom when I heard the shot. It’s my prostate. I can’t make it through the night without a couple trips. Betsy’s cabin is right outside the window. I was at her door in under a minute. A few other people came out after I did. We pounded on the door and when we didn’t get a response I called 911.’

‘And your name, sir?’

‘Walter Jaeger. Navy, retired. Cabin 6.’

‘When you heard the shot, did you look out the bathroom window?’

‘It’s a frosted pane and it hasn’t opened since my son-in-law painted the trim.’

I climb three steps to the front porch of cabin 5. ‘Mrs. Warren,’ I call, rapping briskly on the door. ‘Sheriff’s Department.’

‘I’ve done all that,’ says Mr. Jaeger.

‘Do you know if she owns guns?’

‘Her husband had the usual assortment of hunting rifles, but since he died they’ve been gathering dust in the rack.'

'Any hand guns that you know of?'

'I doubt it.'

I remove my shoes outside the door. The door knob wobbles and almost comes off in my hand. I pull out a credit card and work it between the frame and the door until the tongue slips into the lock. I unsnap the holster at my hip and instruct the onlookers to move back about twenty feet. Slowly and carefully I push the door inward.

'Sheriff's Department. Coming in,' I say. 'Don't be alarmed, Mrs. Warren.'

I step inside and wave my flashlight beam through the interior gloom. The form of a small grey-haired woman in a flannel nightgown is lying half off the bed. She's face down, her head only inches above a pool of blood congealing on the floorboards. I don't need to check her pulse to know she's dead. I use my handkerchief to switch on the overhead light, then go from room to room with gun drawn.

When I'm satisfied that I'm alone I holster my gun and approach the bed.

There's a large exit wound at the back of the victim's skull so I know she's been shot in the face. I find no weapon in proximity to the body. I see a .45 caliber cartridge on the floor beside the bed, draw a chalk circle around it and leave it for the crime scene analysts.

I step outside and call Cappy over. 'The lady's gone. We need to get the coroner's team out here.'

'Suicide?' he asks.

'Homicide. She was shot point blank.'

'The door was locked.'

'The shooter locked it on his way out.'

'Are you saying this was a hit?' he says.

'You could call it that.'

'We don't have hits on Little Papoose Lake.'

'Call it what you will.

'Let me make myself useful. I can put in the call to the coroner.'

'I'd appreciate it.'

'I can secure the perimeter if you point me to the crime tape. I hate rolling out of bed for nothing.'

'Thanks, Cap. It's in the glove box.'

I go back inside and close the door. It's

your typical vacation cabin, a main room with a small kitchenette and bath, a few dying embers glowing in the stone fireplace. There's a small television and an old upright piano with a hymn book sitting on the bench. The residence hasn't been tossed. There are no up-ended drawers, no contents scattered about. Whoever did this had the wherewithal to remove their shoes and enter in their stocking feet.

On the coffee table is a newspaper. I lean over for a closer look. It's turned to Sterling Seabright's obituary, the name of the mortuary underlined in blue ink. The announcement is accompanied by a photo of Sterling standing beside the grey horse I saw in Eddie's painting. She's holding a blue ribbon. She has a big smile on her face. On the bed stand is a copy of James Patterson's *1st To Die*, except Betsy Warren is not the first to die.

We have two murder victims in the span of a week in a place where our most frequent crimes involve drunk and disorderlies, poaching game or using profanity in the presence of women and children, a one-hundred-year-old law that's virtually unenforceable, since kids are doing most of the cussing. I wrap my arms around myself, the pre-dawn chill finding its way through my clothes. There's a knock at the door and Frack steps inside. He's already removed his shoes.

'I'm glad you're here,' I say.

'I was in the shower when the call came in.'

'We have another homicide on our hands.'

He closes the door and looks at the woman slumped over the side of the bed.

'Who is she?'

'Betsy Warren. Unless she's leaving a fortune to an heir who thinks she's taking too long to die, I can't think of a motive for shooting a harmless old woman.' Frack steps further into the room and looks around.

'If this was a robbery the guns would be gone,' he says, looking at the wall rack, heavy with rifles and shotguns. 'The first thing thieves go for are guns, money, jewelry and electronics. There's nothing here to take. Her TV has got to be twenty years old for cris'sake.'

'Not exactly a burglar's paradise. Whoever walked in that door came with one objective, to kill Mrs. Warren. But why?'

Frack looks down at the newspaper and sees the same thing I did. 'She underlined Sterling Seabright's obituary.'

'I noticed that.'

'I wonder if it means anything?'

'It's a small town. She may have known her.'

Paula Dennison arrives as the first responders are pulling out. I wave my thanks from the porch.

'Come on in, Paula. We've got another one for you.'

'Two in a week? In Abundance, this is a crime wave.'

I bring her up to speed. 'We'll get out of your way so you can process the scene. Nothing's been touched, so it's just the way you like it. There's a cartridge beside the bed and a bullet somewhere in the bedding.'

Frack and I are halfway out the door when we hear a pitiful meow and a fat orange cat peeks from beneath the bed. He's terrified, his fur puffed out, his eyes like big gold moons.

'Whoops,' I say. 'Looks like we missed something.' He lets me pick him up. Back on the porch Frack gets into his shoes. He holds the cat so I can get into mine, then hands him back to me. The cold has driven most of the onlookers back to their cabins. Mr. Jaeger is standing under his porch overhang smoking a cigarette and we walk over.

'She's dead, isn't she,' he says.

'I'm afraid so, Mr. Jaeger. This is my partner Frank Tilsley.' They acknowledge one another with a handshake.

'Excuse me while I look around outside,' says Frack, walking back toward 5.

'I never would have made her for a suicide,' says Jaeger. 'Just yesterday she was telling us a joke she heard on Leno.'

'This is a homicide.'

'Murder? That's impossible!'

'It might be impossible, but it's still true.'

The cat reaches out a paw to Mr.

Jaeger and Walter scratches him between the ears. 'I'm glad Tigger's okay,' he says. 'They're both an institution around here.'

'My plate is full right now, Mr. Jaeger. My partner and I are working two homicides and we have two officers out on medical leave. I can't leave Tigger in the cabin and I'd hate to see him go to the shelter.'

'I'll take him,' he says, lifting him from my arms. 'My wife Shirley loves all furry creatures as long as they're not spiders.' The cat settles in his arms and starts to tread the sleeve of his robe.

Frack returns after a few minutes. 'Hannibal's army has already tracked through the mud. We can forget about any relevant footprints.'

'Concerned neighbors,' I say. 'No one was thinking crime scene'.

'How did she get along with her neighbors?' asks Frack.

'Just fine. She played piano, baked cookies, liked to chat. I don't know what else to tell you. She lived on Social Security and didn't have two red cents to rub together.'

'What about next of kin?'

'She was the last of the Mohicans,' says Jaeger. 'She was eighty-nine and outlived all three of her children.'

'Has anyone been hanging around who doesn't belong out here? Any suspicious activity?'

'No. Things get real quiet once school starts.'

'So, it's unlikely she witnessed a drug deal or something of that nature.'

'Highly unlikely.'

'We'll be back in the morning,' I tell him. 'Maybe someone knows something that hasn't bubbled to the surface yet.'

'I'll be here.' He runs his hand over the cat's back. 'Come by the cabin for coffee in the morning. Shirley puts the pot on at seven.'

15

My pager rings before I make it to the truck. I listen for less than twenty seconds.

'We're on our way,' I say, breaking into a run. 'A girl is being attacked between the biker bar and the trailer court,' I tell Frack. 'The state police are on their way, but we're closest to the scene.' As I pull away from the cabins, he's already blazing the trail in front of me.

We barrel down the highway through the dark woods, the magnetic eye spinning on the roof of the truck. We clatter over the bridge that spans the Little Papoose, Gladys's Bar a flash of green neon through the trees.

We speed through the empty streets of the business district and come out on the far end of town, leaving the last streetlight behind. Beyond the biker bar, the crumbled sidewalks morph into a dirt path that twists through a field of weeds toward the back of an exhausted trailer court.

As we slide to a stop we capture the assault in the crossbeam of our headlights. A girl fights for her life against a man three times her size. With one hand he grabs the back of her leather belt, the other hand clutching her long blonde hair next to the scalp. He lifts her off her feet and carries her into the field.

Frack bolts from his truck and runs into the field with me at his heels. He drives a bunched fist into the man's right kidney and the girl tumbles to the ground. I slam my baton into the back of the man's knees and he folds like a cheap lawn chair. Frack pulls his left arm behind his back and snaps a cuff on the wrist. I get my cuff on the other one, but as we attempt to join the two sets behind his back, he pulls from my grasp and I catch an elbow in the face. I let out a yelp, but recapture the arm and connect the cuffs.

Frack flashes me a concerned look. 'I'm okay!' I tell him.

He drags the hulk to his feet. He's over

six feet tall and weighs three hundred pounds if he weighs an ounce, his body adorned in leather and chains, every inch of visible skin inked with symbols of defiance. Frack yanks him to the shoulder of the road, kicks his feet out from under him and watches him come down hard on his butt.

I kneel beside the girl, who lies shaking and sobbing on the ground. Her face is battered and bruised. She's young and very petite, the top buttons ripped from her jean jacket, her flip-flops scattered on the path.

'My thumb!' she cries, holding out her hand. It's twisted at the joint, purpling and swollen to twice its normal size.

'You're going to be okay. The medics are on their way.'

'No! I can't go to the hospital. My mom doesn't have the money.'

'You can't worry about that right now. What's your name?'

'Karen Patterson.'

'How old are you?'

'Fourteen.'

I help her to her feet and brush her

skirt down. 'Let me look at you.' Her left eye is swollen shut. Blood is dripping from her nose. I hand her my handkerchief. She presses it to her nose. Despite the tears in her eyes she looks at me and sputters a laugh.

'What?' I say. She points to my face. I touch it with the tips of my fingers.

My left eye is swollen shut and blood drips from my nose down the front of my jacket. We're the mirror image of one another.

'I guess that *is* funny,' I say. 'Can you walk?'

'I'll be okay,' she says. 'I've had worse.'

'What do you mean?'

'My mom's boyfriend used to work me over, but he's in jail now.'

'Good. He needs to stay there. What are you doing on the street at this hour? It'll be light soon.'

'I was sleeping at my friend's house, but her parents started fighting and throwing things. They'd both been drinking and I got scared. I'd have called home but our phone's been disconnected. It was only three blocks to the trailer court and I thought, what can possibly go wrong in three blocks?'

The first responders arrive. They hand me a wad of damp paper towels for my nose and take charge of the girl. A state police car pulls to the curb and state trooper Harry Fiegel gets out. He's in his mid-thirties with prematurely grey hair and mismatched eyes, one brown and one green. A guy in middle school got his lights punched out when he said Harry's mom had sex with two guys in the same night and that's why his eyes came out the way they did.

'Geez, it's good to see you Harry,' I say.

'I heard about Mike. I guess it's down to just you and Frank. Unless you want me to butt out, I can help fill the void.'

'Yes please. We're already working two homicides and now an attempted sexual assault of a minor. She fits the general age and physical description of our first victim. I'm afraid we've got a lot of knots to untangle and not enough fingers.'

'What's the other case? I thought there was only one.'

'An elderly woman. It happened just

hours ago at the lake. I'll fax you over the particulars.'

'And you want me to see if the cases are connected.'

'Yes, I want to know if the biker is good for the Seabright case.'

'I can work that angle. I can start by taking Godzilla off your hands.'

'Pin down this guy's movements on both sides of midnight on Thursday.'

'The window for the Seabright homicide?'

'That's right, and keep in mind he may have a fetish for young, long-haired blondes.'

'Who doesn't?'

'Git outta here, Harry.'

Cappy Hendricks walks over. 'We've got to stop meeting like this,' he says.

'I knew you were going to say that. How's Karen doing?'

'The ambulance is on its way. We've sent someone to get her mother.'

'What's the situation with her thumb?'

'Bad. It looks like she put it on backward.'

'Ouch!'

He heads back to the truck and I join Harry and Frack. The biker looks up at me from his spot at the curb, his eyes droopy and unfocused. From three feet away his breath is incendiary and I retreat a couple steps. If he lights a cigarette he'll blow his face off.

Harry looks down at the detainee. 'I think your perp's motorcycle is parked outside Buba's. The tags are expired.'

'Good. Impound it,' says Frack, giving the hulk a knuckle-rap on the head to get his attention. 'Do you remember my question? Just think. It'll come to you.'

'I'm trying,' he mumbles. 'I knew it just a minute ago.'

'Knew what?' I ask.

'His name,' says Frack.

'Oh great!'

16

Madison wakes early and goes down to the kitchen to finish the diary before the rest of the family is up. There are only a few paragraphs to go, and in truth, she's beginning to lose interest in the narrative. She puts peanut butter on a piece of dry bread and nibbles at it while she reads.

We slip away to the cabin or a motel, but now that I need him to stick by me, I doubt his commitment, or lack thereof.

The cabin? The motel? It isn't smart to go all the way when you're only seventeen years old and still in school. Life's complicated enough without sneaking around and taking a lot of risks. It doesn't sound like the relationship is going all that well either. One thing's for sure. Sterling isn't the little angel Martha Seabright thinks she is.

We need to have a serious conversation, but he's not a talker, especially when it comes to things he doesn't want to hear.

Eddie not a talker? That doesn't sound right. You can't shut Eddie up. He talks with words, with hands, with a paint-brush, with graceful on-stage body language. He speaks not only his words, but Shakespeare's and Ibsen's and Pirandello's. It's one of the things Madison loved about him. They never ran out of interesting conversation.

I don't like E.B. as much as I liked C. He's not who I thought he was or I wouldn't have allowed myself to get involved in such an intimate way. When I'm with him I can't stand him. When I'm away from him I want to be with him. I guess I'm pretty confused right now. I thought we had more than a physical connection; that we could look forward to a real future. That's what he led me to believe. Now, he's pulling away and I'm stranded on an island with no one to talk to.

And that's where the diary ends. The rest of the pages are blank.

Madison slaps the book closed, tosses it

in her bag and heads out the door. She'd hoped to satisfy her curiosity, to achieve a sense of vindication or closure, but poking into Sterling's most private thoughts leaves her empty and sad. For all her beauty and privilege Sterling wasn't a very happy person in her final days. *I'm no longer the girl I was at the Blue Hole*, she'd written of herself. She could have used a friend, except she'd driven away the ones who cared for her most.

Madison tosses her unchewable piece of bread to the chickens, stops to tie a loose shoe lace and runs for the school bus.

★ ★ ★

The next morning I load Fargo and his water bowl into the roomy space behind the driver's seat. I set the revolving light on the roof of the cab, the magnetic sheriff's logo 'To Serve and Protect' on the doors, and meet Frack at the lake.

The Jaegers are up and invite us in for coffee.

Shirley's a friendly, energetic woman,

enjoying her comfortable retirement years. I can tell she's a cat lover when I see Tigger on the counter licking bacon grease from the frying pan.

'What happened to you?' she says, setting the sugar bowl in front of me. 'You go twelve rounds with Mike Tyson?'

'My face can't look *that* bad.'

'Oh, is that what it is?'

Everyone laughs including myself.

'After last night I'm cutting my sleep medication in half,' says Shirley, sipping her coffee. 'I can't believe I slept through all the excitement. The gunshot. The sirens. The flashing lights. And all of it right next door.' She settles into the chair across from mine. 'I'm going to miss Betsy. She was a harmless old woman, clever and funny. Maybe the killer thought she was someone else, like a case of mistaken identity.'

'Like a former tenant?' says Frack. 'How long has she lived there?'

'Since Adam and Eve were kicked out of the Garden of Eden,' says Walter. 'You're barking up the wrong tree on that one.'

'You know there is something I remember,' says Shirley. 'It probably doesn't mean anything, but Betsy told us that on Friday she saw a man and woman exit Cabin 4 at dawn.'

'We're talking about 4 now, not 5. Am I correct?' I say.

'That's right.'

'Was it supposed to be vacant or what?' says Frack, stirring sugar into his coffee.

'Betsy kept an eye on 4 for the owners who use it only in the summer. Anyone they give permission to stay there is supposed to call Betsy so she can get it ready.'

'And no one called this time.'

'That's right,' says Walter. 'I didn't think to mention that. The Mortons in 3 used to keep an eye on the place, but they went into foreclosure and moved, so Betsy took over. The owners pay her a little to keep the place tidied up.'

'Who are the owners?'

'That would be Brock and Jean Breyer,' says Shirley. 'They live twenty minutes away in New London.'

Breyer. Frack and I exchange a glance.

'New London?' says Frack. 'Not on Stonebridge in Abundance?'

'No, that would be somebody else.' Shirley writes the number down on a grocery receipt and hands it to him. 'In case you want to call them.' We chat a while longer, thank them for their hospitality and go back outside.

Frack calls the Breyers from the porch of 5 while Fargo and I take a stroll on the grounds. A young man with a full, nicely trimmed beard comes out of a cabin down the row and walks up to me. He wears scarred steel-toed boots, jeans and a white cable-knit sweater over a red plaid shirt. The only thing missing is an ax and a Blue Ox. He tells me his name is Jim Flint and I tell him I'm Robely Danner.

'Where did you find Dog?' he says, gesturing toward Fargo.

'Is he yours?' I ask, patting Fargo's head and feeling a sudden twinge of separation anxiety.

'He was the Arnsides' dog.'

'The Arnsides?'

'Jed and Peg. They spent a month here. They tried to give the dog away, but he doesn't herd or hunt, so there weren't any takers. I don't think he'll make much of a police dog either.'

'So where are the Arnsides now?'

'Back in Chicago. The day after they left I saw Dog on the side of the highway and knew they'd ditched him. He waited right where they left him like he thought they were coming back. Every time I got close he ran into the woods and I'd leave food by the trunk of a tree. When I didn't see him anymore, I thought a car got him.'

'I don't get it. He's a great dog.'

'By the time he grew into those paws he was bigger than their apartment in the city.'

'Did they say how old he is?'

'About 14 months.'

'I guess I can keep him then. I'm glad we bumped into each other.'

'What do you call him?'

'Fargo, like the movie. He deserves something better than Dog, don't you think?'

'Cool name. I like that. Are you single?'

The abrupt detour in the conversation

catches me off guard. 'I'm involved,' I say, after a brief pause.

'Well, let me know if your status changes. I'd love to date a lady with a nice set of handcuffs,' he says, with a playful wink. As Flint gets in his vehicle and heads toward the main road, Fargo walks through the trees to explore the shoreline.

The Breyers arrive in a new Lexus. Frack and I introduce ourselves. They're an older couple. Brock has faded ginger hair and friendly rounded features. Jean is a thin bird-boned woman in a puffy purple coat and a knit hat with ear flaps. More than one resident of the lake has notified them about the shooting. Like everyone else they're shocked and bewildered at the news.

'Everyone loved Betsy,' says Jean. 'She was a dyed-in-the-wool Lutheran, you know. Played the piano in church every Sunday.'

'Shirley said Betsy saw two people leaving your cabin on Friday morning. Do you know who they might have been?'

'Not really. When extended family

wants to use it, they're supposed to call first. It was in the pre-dawn hour, so between that and her bad eyesight she couldn't give details, only that there was a man and a woman who was his height or taller.'

'Anything else?'

'The girl had light hair that stood out in the semi-darkness. That's about all she said.'

'How about a car?'

'They left on foot,' says Brock. 'If there was a car it was parked on the highway.'

'Do they sound like anyone you know?'

'No one comes to mind. Nothing was damaged or stolen so there was no need to report it.'

'How many people have keys to the place?'

'A few family members. The Mortons forgot to leave theirs when they moved, and of course, Betsy had one that she frequently misplaced. We don't worry that much about security. There's never been any trouble at the lake. I guess last night changes everything.'

'Would you object if we had a look

inside?' asks Frack.

'Are you thinking this couple had something to do with Betsy's murder?' says Jean.

'Not necessarily, but we don't want to leave any stones unturned,' I say.

'You don't mind if they have a look around, do you Jean?' says Brock.

'No, of course not,' she says.

'Follow me, Mr. Breyer. I'd like to show you something,' I say.

'I'll wait in the car where it's warm,' says Jean.

Frack and Breyer follow me onto the porch of number 4. I take my credit card and open the door in the same manner I accessed Mrs. Warren residence.

'That's pretty slick,' says Brock.

'How old is the cabin, Mr. Breyer?'

'Oh, fifty years or so.'

'So is the door knob. I suggest you replace it with a modern lock set with a deadbolt. This little piece of plastic is all it takes for anyone to enter your cabin, or Mrs. Warren's.'

'Thank you. That's good advice and I intend to take it. I'll be in the car with

Jean if you need me.'

At one time the cabins were owned by a single party who had them built to the same blueprint. Since then the complex has been divided up and sold to various individuals. Some are used exclusively by the owners, others used as income property. The Breyers' cabin has stylish log furniture, guns and hunting bows in locked racks, the head of a moose above the door and a prehistoric-looking sturgeon mounted above the mantle. This is, after all, Wisconsin.

'Did that lumberjack make a pass at you?' says Frack, as soon as we're alone.

'He wasn't all that serious,' I say, looking around the room. 'He simply asked if I was single.'

'What did you tell him?'

'I told him I was involved.' I search Frack's face. 'That's true isn't it? We are involved, aren't we?'

'I am,' he says.

'Good.' I walk across the room and pull down the bed covers. The sheets are pristine, not a stain, strand of hair, bobby pin or wrinkle. I make it up again. 'I think

Betsy tidied up after the couple left.'

'She missed something on the sink,' calls Frack, from the bathroom. He holds up three long blonde hairs and bags them. We're both thinking the same thing. There are no cigarette butts, empty beer cans, pizza boxes or clutter on the kitchen counter tops to indicate kids crashing the place to party. Betsy was a chatterbox. If the cabin had been a mess she would have told the Jaegers. The couple who stayed here was looking for one thing. A quiet place to rendezvous.

I squint at the hairs through the glassine envelope. 'Sterling Seabright,' I say.

'Maybe. Let's hope there's a root for DNA testing. Right now they're just generic blonde hairs.'

'Our cases could very well be connected. Betsy recognized Sterling in the newspaper photo as having a general likeness to the girl she saw leaving here. That's why she underlined the obituary. She's dead because she saw something she wasn't supposed to see or knew something she wasn't supposed to know.'

'That's a possibility,' says Frack. 'If it was Sterling she may have been here with Eddie Breyer. E.B. He's certainly strong enough to have committed the murder and I bet you anything he's related to Brock and Jean.'

'Oh please! Eddie couldn't kill anyone. You said so yourself.'

'I was being facetious.'

'His grief was palpable, Frack.'

'He's an actor, remember? He has an androgynous sensuality that could easily jump the gender gap. Ask Madison Buckley. She was certainly drawn to him. Maybe he swings from both trees. And just because he's gay doesn't mean he isn't capable of getting a girl pregnant.'

'She wasn't pregnant!'

'She didn't know that, and if she didn't know that, the guy she was getting it on with wouldn't have known it either.'

'Okay, let's test our theory. We'll show Brock Breyer the knife and see if there's a reaction.' We lock the door and walk to the Lexus. Mr. Breyer gets out and shuts the door.

'How did it go?' he says. 'Was it

Goldilocks and the three bears?'

'I don't know, but at least they weren't vandals out to trash the place,' I say. 'Do you know if Betsy cleaned up after the squatters left?'

'I can't say for sure, but she's somewhat of a neat freak. She would probably have tidied up and laundered the bedding.'

'I notice several Breyers in the phone book,' says Frack. 'You wouldn't be related to the family on Stonebridge would you?'

'We're all apples from the same tree if you go back far enough, but yes, that's where our grandson Eddie lives. He's a very talented artist. It's a shame Eldron doesn't appreciate the boy.'

'Eldron? Who's Eldron?' I ask.

'Our son. Eddie's father. Everyone calls him Coach, sometimes El, but never Eldron. He hates his name. We combined the names of my brothers, Elder and Ronald. Jean and I thought it was oh so clever at the time, but not so much anymore.'

E.B. Eddie Breyer. Eldron Breyer.

'We met him. He's the gym teacher, right? The basketball guy,' I say.

'That's right.'

I take the miniature jack-knife from my pocket and show it to Brock.

'Have you seen this before?' I ask. 'You can barely make out the initials.'

'E.B.? It could be El's. I guess that solves the riddle of the mystery intruder,' he says, assuming we recovered it from the cabin. He extends his hand. 'I'll give it to him in church on Sunday.'

I drop it back in my pocket and see a flicker of surprise on his face. 'I'll return it at the Seabright funeral,' I say. 'I have to touch bases with him anyway.'

I see his wheels turning. The knife. The blonde girl. The funeral. I see the shift in Mr. Breyer's demeanor, the hint of fear in his eyes. 'On second thought I can't be sure,' he says. This time his voice has a little catch in it. 'Those initials look more like B.B. It could even be mine. I just can't remember.'

17

Madison walks down the sidewalk to the sheriff's station. It's a cold, wet morning and she has no coat to cover her thin cotton dress. It's time to part with the diary, but she's not sure that giving it to the Seabrights, with all its intimate revelations, is the right thing to do. She's not crazy about Martha, but she doesn't want to hurt her either. She'll hand it to Officer Danner and let her decide what's best. She'll say that Sterling forgot it at her house. No one can prove otherwise.

The door is locked and the blinds are pulled over the windows. Madison rattles the door, but there's no one inside. If she hangs around until someone arrives she'll be late for class. She decides to hand the diary over to Mr. Gregory instead. She walks toward school, hunger grinding away inside her, the morning chill sinking into her bones.

* * *

'Brock Breyer knows something about his son that we don't,' I say, as Frack and I walk through the trees and down the slope to the lake. We find Fargo sleeping in a green rowboat. 'It's obvious he adores his talented grandson, but he only mentioned Eldron as a footnote and not in the most glowing terms. Normally one would say, 'that's where my son lives,' but he said 'that's where my grandson lives.''

'He doesn't like the way Eldron treats Eddie, but that doesn't mean Brock is ready to throw Eldron under the bus,' says Frack.

'If Eddie and Sterling were close friends, Eldron would have at least known who she was. Whether there was more to it than that is something we need to look into. I want to know what his alibi is for the night of the homicide.'

'We still can't nail down Carl's alibi . . . watching TV when his parents left . . . sleeping when they got home. And just because he and Sterling broke up doesn't mean they weren't friends with benefits,' says Frack. 'That was one question he refused to answer. What if they were friends with benefits?'

'I hate that expression,' I say, 'but, you're right. He's holding something back. Madison Buckley is holding back too. Adolescents live in a universe unto themselves and we adults are alien imposters. Add the cop clothes and badges to the equation and I'm surprised they talk to us at all.'

'For now I'm putting the biker at the top of the list,' says Frack. 'Karen Patterson and our murder victim look like sisters. That's too much coincidence for me. He's a violent recidivist and men like that don't change.'

'Let's see what Harry comes up with.'

Wind sweeps the surface of the lake and the boat rocks gently on the ripples, Fargo snoring softly in his sleep. 'I've never known a dog to sleep this much,' I say. 'Maybe he has tired blood.'

'It's because he's still growing,' says Frack.

'Take that back,' I say, laughing. 'Dogs don't get much bigger than this, do they?'

'Come on,' he says, slipping his arm around my waist. 'Let's walk up the shore and enjoy the colors. The trees are already past peak.'

'Sure, why not.' We head up the pebbly shore. Little Papoose Lake is five hundred acres of sparkling blue water created ten thousand years ago by receding ice-age glaciers. It's ringed with spicy groves of evergreen and blazing stands of maple and oak shedding gold and scarlet leaves into the wind. Any day now it will be frozen over with ice-fishing shacks scattered across its surface like dice on a gaming table.

'I have some good news,' I say. 'Fargo was abandoned. I get to keep him.'

'Who told you that, the Merry Woodsman?'

'Yes.' I give him a friendly punch on the arm. 'You sound jealous.'

'So, now he's yours?'

'Yes, the dog, not the woodsman.'

'Is that a good thing?'

'Of course it is. You know how quickly I get attached to warm, cuddly creatures.'

'I hope that includes me,' he says.

'I think we both know the answer to that.'

'Do we? Does that mean we're going together?' he asks. 'I like to know where I stand. Loose ends make me edgy.'

'Me too. I like things tied up in a neat bow. Would *you* like to go together? *I* would,' I say.

'I'd like that too.'

'Exclusively?' I ask. 'I'm not into sexual multi-tasking. Gladys has already cornered the market on that one.'

'Exclusive is the word I had in mind. That's what going together means . . . doesn't it?' he says.

'That's what it means to me. Last night was a pretty big commitment on my part,' I tell him. 'As far as I'm concerned that seals the deal.'

He pulls me into his embrace. The wind whips up and we find ourselves standing in a churning vortex of bright leaves.

'You look happy,' he says.

'I am.'

'Do you feel better after we talked last night?'

'It was a beginning. It helped me put things in perspective.' He kisses me on top of the head.

'Good. Come on, let's go solve a crime.'

* * *

When we leave the lake, Frack and I go in separate directions. He heads to Calumet Road where a young doe is tangled in a barbed wire fence. On my way to the station I stop to see Tammy and grab a turkey sandwich. She looks at me with her mouth open.

'Don't say it! I caught an elbow in the face. And don't tell Mike. It looks worse than it is.'

'It's driving Mike crazy being out of the loop,' she says, 'but as of this morning, he's lucky to make it to the bathroom without passing out.'

'I'll call him as soon as I get a minute. Tammy, you're somewhat of a social networker. Does the name Eldron Breyer ever come up in conversation?'

'Eldron . . . you mean Coach? Come to

think of it, there was some kind of buzz when he first came to town.'

'Do you remember what it was about?'

'No one understood why he left a higher paying position in Green Bay for less pay in Abundance. He said it was because his parents lived nearby in New London, but somebody said he and his folks aren't that close.'

'I hear his late wife had money. Maybe he could afford the cut in pay.'

'How about I poke around, make a few calls to my gossipy friends. What is it you're looking for exactly?'

'Dirt. Start digging.'

* * *

Back at the station a man is waiting outside the door with a purse under his arm.

'I'm Deputy Danner. May I help you, sir?'

'I'm John Pit. I own the Fire Pit Bar in Ogdensburg. I found this in the alley trash can. Judging from the driver's license, it belonged to that pretty young murder victim whose picture is in the paper.'

'Ogdensburg?'

'Yes, ma'am.'

It sounds like the murderer may have continued south for another ten miles after the attack, ditched the purse, then horseshoed into Abundance the back way. It's one possible scenario among a dozen others.

'I suppose you didn't see who put it there.'

'No ma'am, but considering the bottles dumped on top of it, it was a couple of days ago. Whoever killed her wasn't after the money. It's still in the wallet.' He can't stop staring at my face.

'I know,' I say. 'I've already been told how frightening I look.'

'How did it happen?

'It was unintentional. I got in the way of an elbow the size of an Easter ham.'

'Imagine what you'd look like if it was on purpose.'

'I'd rather not go there.'

'I mean no offense, but I don't think

ladies belong in law enforcement. It's too dangerous.'

'It was law enforcement or working the spigots at my mom's bar.'

He squints at me. 'You're not little Robely, Gladys Calhoun's daughter?'

'Bingo.'

'In that case I'm glad you chose the safer route.'

When we're through laughing I shuffle through the contents of the purse. No cell phone.

'Mr. Pit, we're stretched thin right now. I'd like to ask a favor of you.'

'Shoot.'

'Check the garbage can again and look around the alley. The victim had a cell phone that hasn't surfaced. It has a black glass front and a pink rubber case. Her mother said if I found the purse, I'd find the phone, but it's not here.'

'The garbage was hauled off, but I'll check the alley. I can also post a note on the bulletin board at the bar.'

'I'd appreciate it. What do you know about Tyson Wetzel? I hear he's one of your regulars.'

'You must have heard about his birthday party. He passed out in the parking lot on top of what was left of his birthday cake.'

'The way he hits the booze it may be his last. How about violent tendencies?'

'He likes to posture, but I've never known him to get physical.'

'Thanks for bringing in the purse, Mr. Pit. We need more good citizens like you.'

I sit at the desk with the pulse beating in my swollen eye, tapping a pen on the desktop, my temples throbbing. The only suspects we can exclude with any certainly are Eddie Breyer and Madison Buckley. He was on stage and she lacked the physical stature to commit the crime. She did however suspect that something was wrong before the body was discovered, as did Hammond. We have yet to explore Eldron Breyer's connection to the deceased, if indeed there was one, and now that Sterling's purse has been discovered behind the Fire Pit, we have to take a closer look at Tyrone Wetzel.

I dump the contents of the purse on the desk and pick through the items one by one. There's forty-three dollars and change in the wallet. If Wexler had been in possession of it, he'd have cleaned it out. A man of his proclivities wouldn't have been able to stop himself. I find a Visa card and an appointment card for Planned Parenthood in Appleton. Her appointment was at 2:30, four days before the murder. Information attained from that visit could provide as much valuable information as the phone, maybe more.

I know I'm pushing the envelope, but I call the clinic and identify myself. I'm transferred to a physician's assistant and explain the circumstances surrounding my inquiry. I ask if he remembers Sterling Seabright.

'I'm sure you're acquainted with our privacy policy,' he says.

I didn't need 20/20 vision to see that coming.

'I think Miss Seabright would be more concerned about catching the person who left her strangled in the woods than about your privacy policy.'

I sit through several beats of silence.

'She's really dead? You've got to be kidding.'

'Check the obits. It's true.'

'When did this occur?'

'Late Friday night. It's a matter of public record. I could subpoena her file, but the more cooperation I get, the quicker we'll get this case resolved.' I sit quietly as he weighs the needs of bureaucracy against the needs of humanity. 'Please, help me with this.'

There's another pause, followed by an impatient sigh. 'One moment.' He says it like he's being dragged to the gallows. He puts the phone on speaker and clicks away at his computer. While I wait I continue rummaging through the purse. I unzip a pink plastic makeup bag and find what I've been looking for, a half empty card of birth control pills. Miss Seabright had tried to do the responsible thing and must have been very confused and frightened when she thought the pills had failed her.

'Okay, here we go,' he says. 'Miss Seabright was scheduled for a pregnancy test. When she was signing in at the desk, she saw a woman pull into the parking lot. It was someone she knew and she immediately left out the back door. We never heard from her again.'

'Did she come in alone? Was there a boy with her?'

'I didn't see anyone, but that doesn't mean he couldn't have been waiting in the car.'

'She thought she was pregnant. Did she mention a name in regard to paternity?'

'Deputy, I'm already walking on thin ice here. Like I said, she was in and out like she was caught in a revolving door.'

'Had you prescribed birth control pills on a previous occasion?'

Click.

I check my watch and give Mike a call. I bring him up to speed on everything . . . what we know, what we think we know and what we don't know, the third category being the largest. 'Harry Fiegel booked the biker for us,' I tell him.

'Oh yeah, the guy with two dads.'

'Stop that, Mike! That's a terrible thing to say.'

'I know, I know, I just couldn't let it

pass.' He laughs until his hilarity ends in a coughing jag.

'Serves you right,' I say. 'I miss you, Big Bear. It's not the same around here without you.'

'I can't wait to get back so I can get some rest. The triplets are maniacs.'

'You mean the ones with the three dads?'

'Alright, I had that coming.'

'Yes, you did. I suggest earplugs and three little straightjackets until you're back on the job.'

That gets a laugh.

'I guess you're riding with Frack until I get back.'

'He's pulling his weight and half of mine, Mike. He's a damn good cop.'

'I know, but is he behaving himself?'

'Mike, Mike, Mike, if Frack was behaving he wouldn't be Frack, now would he?'

18

By the time Madison arranges an appointment with Mr. Gregory it's almost lunchtime. Mrs. Finch has her take a seat in the waiting room outside his office door, then goes down the hall to photocopy a stack of papers. The door is ajar and Madison hears scraps of conversation coming from inside. She scoots her chair closer to the door.

'I hesitated coming to you with this,' says a voice she can't quite place. 'I thought of taking it to Sheriff Brooker or Mike Oxenburg, but decided to run it by you first.'

'What's on your mind, Coach? I have an appointment with a student in five minutes.'

Coach Breyer. Now she recognizes the voice.

'It's in regard to the Hammond boy.'

'Carl?'

'Yes, sir.'

Madison leans closer to the door.

'He's our star player, isn't he?' says Gregory.

'The best we've got. That's why I gave this a lot of thought before coming here.'

'Gave what a lot of thought?'

'Carl came to me over a week ago with some unsettling concerns. He thought he'd gotten a girl in trouble.'

'What kind of trouble?'

'*That* kind of trouble'

'Hmm, I see.'

'At least, that's what *she* told *him*. I suggested he confide in his parents or his pastor,' says Coach.

'And did he?'

'I don't think so. Then a few days ago he told me to forget about the conversation, that everything had been taken care of. He used those very words. Taken care of.'

'That settles it then. It was a tempest in a tea cup. These things often are.'

'That's what I thought until I heard that Sterling Seabright had been murdered. One might say she'd been taken care of . . . permanently.'

The conversation stutters to a stop. 'Oh, for heaven's sake! Certainly, you're not implying . . . '

'Just wait a minute. Consider this. They went together all last year and his name has never come up in relation to anyone else, nor has hers. There might be nothing to it, but with the timing and everything . . . '

'Are you out of your mind? If she were pregnant, the police would be pounding down my door with a million questions.'

'They still might. Nobody's seen a Death Certificate. We don't know what's on it.'

'I hope you're not implying he had something to do with her demise.'

'Well, I . . . '

'Really El, I've never known you to be this irresponsible. If you've been slandering his name around campus, we could have a lawsuit on our hands.'

'Alright, alright! I overreacted. Let's just forget it.'

'As far as I'm concerned, we never had this conversation, but since we're on the subject of Miss Seabright, she came to see me recently and wanted to know if I'd made a decision regarding her transfer to the boys' basketball team. She thought you'd been advocating with me on her behalf.'

'I don't know what she was thinking, Neville. She came to me with that brainstorm at the beginning of the school year. It was absurd and I told her so. Unfortunately, she's a headstrong young lady, used to having her way.'

'Apparently you failed to get through to her,' says Gregory. 'The people of Abundance aren't ready to see a girl roughed up for the sake of sport. This community would have my head and I wouldn't blame them.'

'What can I say? The girl went over my head.'

After listening to their conversation, the importance of the diary has taken on new dimensions. She's not giving it to Gregory, Danner or anyone else. By the time Coach Breyer leaves the principal's office, Madison Buckley is running across campus in search of Carl.

* * *

When Frack enters the station, his jacket torn, blood leaking through a shredded leather glove, I jump so quickly out of the chair that it hits the wall. I grab my purse and pull him into the restroom by his sleeve. He holds his hand over the sink as I peel away the glove and toss it in the waste can. I run warm water over the wound and gently lather it with liquid soap.

'You have to have this hand looked at,' I say. 'You'll need stitches and a tetanus booster.'

'I got caught up in the barbed wire,' he says, as I rinse off the soap and pat it dry. 'It took two farmers and a pair of wire cutters to get the deer untangled. Do you have any idea how hard a one hundred pound doe can kick?'

'I do. She clipped you on the jaw. It's turning black.'

He looks in the mirror above the sink. 'I was pumping too much adrenaline at the time to feel it.'

While he's examining his chin in the

mirror, I take a bottle of perfume from my purse and splash it over his hand.

'Son-of-a . . . oh, oh, oh!' he says, with a groan. 'Why don't you just set it on fire?'

'Sorry. That'll keep it from getting infected. There's no telling what bacteria you've been exposed to.' I take a clean towel from the cabinet and wrap it around his hand. 'Keep that on until the bleeding stops. Did the doe make it?'

'She was torn up some . . . oh geezus, that stings,' he says, shaking his hand, ' . . . but she bounded into the woods like a long-distance runner.'

'That's good. She'll be okay. So will you.' I give him a reassuring hug.

'Aren't we two beauties?' he says, catching our battered images in the glass.

'We look like total incompetents. I'm glad the chief can't see us. Come sit. I'll pour you a cup of coffee,' I say. 'There were some new developments while you were out.' I tell him about John Pit and the purse, the birth control pills and what I learned from my call to Planned Parenthood. 'I was about to move Wexler to the back burner, but with the purse being tossed behind his favorite watering hole, we can't scratch him off the list,' I say.

'Still no phone though?'

'That was a disappointment, but it's out there somewhere.'

'Last time I looked, somewhere was a big place,' says Frack.

'You're right.'

'Don't forget, the visitation this afternoon. We need to make a showing at the funeral home, but I don't want to get stuck at the church sitting through a two-hour Mass. Are you okay with that?'

'We'll keep it brief. I'll wear my black dress. My only dress actually. Who knows, maybe we'll learn something.'

⋆ ⋆ ⋆

We're about to leave the station when the phone rings and Frack picks up. He covers the mouthpiece. 'It's Harry,' he says, pushing the speaker button.

'Harry,' says Frack. 'What's up with our perp?'

'Well, for starters, his name is Bucky Barnes. When I read it off his expired driver's license it jogged his memory.'

Now we have a second B.B. to go with our two E.B.s. I'm beginning to wish I'd left the knife in the ditch.

'Bucky?' I ask. 'That's his real name?'

'Seems so. We charged him with felony battery and attempted sexual assault on a minor. This is his fourth violent felony, so he'll be locked up for a very long time.'

'It sounds like he should have been locked up already. Has he been convicted of sexual assault before?'

'Arrested twice, but the charges were dropped. Both times he not only knew the victims, but they'd been drinking together. They refused to cooperate so the D.A chose not to pursue it. The women's meth and prostitution histories would have discredited their testimony, but that doesn't mean they weren't telling the truth. Both were long-haired blondes like the Seabright and Patterson girls, but that's where the similarities end.'

'Where was he on Friday night?'

'At 12:07 p.m., he was pushing his

motorcycle along the shoulder of the highway.'

'How can you be that specific?' asks Frack.

'One of our patrolmen helped him get his machine fired up. Barnes was told to renew his license and registration and he was let off with a warning. No one knew at the time that there was a dead body only feet away.'

'Have you grilled him about the Seabright girl?'

'He says he doesn't know there'd been a homicide.'

'When do we get our crack at him?' I ask. 'How about today after the Seabright funeral?'

'Sure, that'll work. Our lab is doing a preliminary on the hairs found on his clothes. By the time you get here we may know something.'

After the call ends, Frack says, 'There's a small window of opportunity there. He could be our guy.'

'A fiber or hair match to our first victim would be useful about now. We've already got him on the Patterson assault. But, if

Barnes is her killer he can't be the man at the cabin. The Seabright girl would never go off with a guy like that.'

'Stranger things have happened.'

'Not *that* strange,' I say, lifting an eyebrow. 'It would have to be someone who knew the cabin was accessible.'

Frack looks at his watch. 'You'd better go get dolled up. I'll get my hand stitched and meet you at the funeral home.'

19

Gregory's reaction was not what Breyer expected. He'd have been better off keeping his big mouth shut. Now he'll be seen as a troublemaker. He grinds his teeth in frustration as he walks across the parking lot. He needs a quiet place to have lunch where he can fortify himself with a couple shots before the funeral. The girl was a troublemaker. He's only going because he doesn't want to be conspicuously absent.

He doesn't see the girls' basketball coach, Mickey Lunn, until she's ambushed him at his car. She rambles on about 'that dear girl', her face red and ugly with weeping. He finds her unfeminine and disgusting with her bulging thighs and runaway caboose.

'Classes are cancelled for the rest of the day, you know. I *will* see you at the funeral, won't I?' she says.

'Yes, of course. I really must go.' Still,

she babbles on until he wants to choke her.

A figure walking purposefully in his direction appears around the corner of the administration building. Even at a distance their eyes lock and he notes the blond hair, the tall stature, the determined, if somewhat gimpy gait. Carl Hammond breaks into a slightly lopsided trot, now a sprint.

How could Carl possibly know what he'd said unless Gregory jumped on the phone the minute he left the office? He feels betrayed on the deepest professional level.

'You'll have to excuse me, Miss Lunn,' he says, his heart climbing into his throat.

Breyer fumbles for his car keys and drops them on the asphalt. As he bends over to pick them up, the first blow lands on the back of his neck and he thumps to his knees. Miss Lunn lets out a burble as Carl kicks Breyer in the ribs, drags him to his feet and lands several resounding slaps to his face and head. With a powerful forearm across the throat, Carl slams him back against the car, the door handle of the white Nissan grinding into his spine.

'What's wrong?' says Coach, covering his head with his arms. 'Are you nuts?'

'I'm calling the cops!' wails Miss Lunn, shocked out of her crying jag.

'No, don't do that!' says Breyer. 'Just go. Please. I can handle this.' She walks backward a few steps, then power-waddles to her car and drives from the lot.

'Look at me, damn it!' says Carl. 'It wasn't me.'

'What?' chokes Breyer.

'It wasn't me. I've been shooting blanks.' He lowers his arm so Coach can breathe. A stunned silence stretches between them. Breyer rubs the angry welts on his face, his cheeks burning with pain and humiliation.

'What?' he says, a second time.

'I have a medical condition. The doctor says I can't get *anyone* pregnant. That makes me wonder why you're so eager to implicate me.'

'It's what you said. I mean, isn't that

what you told me? I thought I was doing the right thing.'

'By tattling to the principal like a gossipy little girl? I'm quitting the team, you pathetic hypocrite. I don't want to be around you anymore.'

'No wait! There's been a terrible misunderstanding here. You know I'd never . . . '

Carl grabs him by the front of his coat, their noses two inches apart.

'Never what? That's what I'm beginning to wonder. Never what, Coach?'

* * *

Frack and I sign the book in the vestibule of Lemke, Schmitt and Cohn Funeral Parlor. Frack looks handsome in a dark, well-tailored suit, a clean bandage on his stitched hand. My black dress was too lacy for the occasion so I changed into black slacks, a beige turtleneck and a black velvet blazer with a silver oak leaf pin on the front. The carpet is blue and cushiony under foot, the air floral-scented, low organ music piped through hidden speakers.

We file by the casket. Sterling is in the lavender gown she was saving for the Christmas dance, her golden hair fanned out on a white satin pillow, the scratches on her face skilfully concealed. She's the princess of fairy tales waiting for a kiss to bring her back to life. Frack and I can't bring her back to life, but we can find the person who took it from her and make sure he pays for his crime.

I dread the thought of parents having to bury their children. There are no words, however well-chosen, to ease the pain. The Seabrights are not young. There will be no more children. They will never laugh in the same spontaneous way, nor embrace one another without the awareness of the grief they share. Martha and Russ graciously accept our condolences. They tell us they're going to be okay, that Sterling is with the Lord in a place of infinite happiness.

'Let's talk,' says Martha. We follow them to a quiet alcove at the back of the room.

'Have you located the man in the white van?' asks Russ.

'We've interviewed him. He's given us his story and we're checking it out,' says Frack.

'Do you think he's the one?'

'It's too early to say, but he has no history of violence toward women.'

'Can you give us his name?'

'You know we can't do that, Mr. Seabright.'

'Afraid I might go after him?'

'I saw the arsenal of hunting rifles in your gun case,' says Frack. 'If I were a suspect and you knew my name I'd be looking over my shoulder.'

'Deputy Tilsley, Russ is far too sensible to do anything foolish,' says Martha. 'It's just that we feel so helpless.'

'I know.'

Russ nods toward Frack's bandaged hand. 'What happened? You're right hand is your good hand, isn't it?'

'It was until a deer got caught in barbwire,' says Frack. 'It took a while to get her free.'

'Mating season. They're all over the

place. That's why our auto insurance rates are so high.'

I've covered my bruises with makeup, but I still look beat up, so I know I'm next.

'What does the other guy look like?' Russ asks.

'Russ!' Martha scolds.

'You mean through the bars at County Jail?' I say. 'Six foot something. Three hundred pounds, give or take a pound or two.'

'Is he the man who killed our daughter?'

'We're questioning him this afternoon. If there's a break in the case, you'll be the first to know.'

'You ladies used to let us fellows do the heavy lifting,' he says. 'What's the world coming to?'

'She likes lifting the paycheck,' says Frack.

'It looks like she earns it,' says Martha.

'Please, excuse me. Mr. Gregory is looking my way.' Russ walks off and Frack goes to check the names in the guest book.

'I hope you'll excuse us if we don't go to the church,' I say, 'but we need to keep going on the case. The first few days are critical.'

'Yes dear, I know. We watch those shows on television,' she says, squeezing my hand. 'I thought of something after you and Deputy Tilsley left. It's probably nothing, but it might be worth mentioning.'

'What is it, Mrs. Seabright?'

'It was the questions about a diary that got me thinking. One evening Sterling was sitting in a chair writing in a book. It had a paisley cloth cover. When I came into the room, she dropped it in her book bag and went upstairs. I didn't think anything of it at the time. I can't find it anywhere in the house. She'd have known better than to write in a textbook, so it had to be a journal.'

'And you're thinking . . . '

'That's what Madison Buckley was after. Maybe Sterling had written something incriminating about her and she didn't want anyone to find out.' It doesn't occur to Martha that Sterling might have had something to hide . . . a common parental blind spot.

'We'll have another talk with Madison. If there's a diary, we need to get our hands on it'.

A short, stocky woman in an ill-fitting pants suit comes toward us. Her face is blotchy, her eyes red and swollen.

'Excuse me, that's Sterling's coach,' says Martha. 'I'd better have a word with her.'

Frack returns from the vestibule with a list of names copied from the guest book. He folds the paper and puts it in his notebook. I tell him about the diary. It's essential we talk with Madison Buckley. The room is filled to capacity, the atmosphere scented with a dizzying mixture of perfume and flowers, each breath of air cycled and recycled.

Eddie and a male friend are standing off to the side near the front of the room. One of the last mourners to appear is Coach Breyer looking slightly rumpled, his face red and swollen. Carl and Madison enter the room ten minutes later. Carl acknowledges me with direct eye contact and a solemn nod. Madison ignores me, but I approach her anyway. I touch her arm so she can't pretend I don't exist.

'Madison,' I say, quietly. 'We really need to talk. When would be a convenient time?'

'I have no legal obligation to talk to you.'

'Yes, I know that, but don't you want to find out who killed your friend? None of us is an island unto herself, Madison. Not me. Not you. We might have a better chance of solving this case if everyone cooperates. That goes for you too, Carl,' I say, looking up at him. 'We're all on the same team, at least we should be.'

'Let me think about it,' says Madison. 'I have a lot on my mind.'

'I'll call you,' says Carl.

'Fair enough, you know where to find me. Just don't wait too long.'

Frack has taken a chair near the back of the room and I sit down next to him.

'Any luck?' he asks.

'I think Carl is ready to cooperate, but that little girl is harder to crack than a walnut.'

'Her science teacher told me she has an incredibly high I.Q. She's working toward a full scholarship to Lawrence College. In the meantime, her parents are threatened with foreclosure and barely keeping the wolf from the door.'

'Looking at the condition of that girl, I'd say the wolf is at the door. I like her, Frack. In her I see a younger me . . . angry . . . distrustful . . . a mother who embarrassed me in public.' I look around the room. 'Did you notice that Coach Breyer and Eddie arrived separately?'

'There's a definite failure to bond,' says Frack, with his usual touch of irony.

A man in a black suit walks to the pulpit at the front of the room. 'It's time for people to give testimonials about the virtues of the deceased.'

'Let's go,' I say. 'I can't breathe in here and my shoes are killing me.'

20

Carl expresses his condolences to the Seabrights. Madison avoids them. She scans the room until her eyes settle on the boy she'd loved and lost, gorgeous Eddie Breyer. Strong, sensitive Eddie. He doesn't at all match the callous portrayal in Sterling's diary. She still wears the silver charm bracelet and the painful scar of rejection on her heart.

Jimi Whitleaf wipes away tears, his head against Eddie's shoulder. Eddie looks as if he'd come from the set of Aida, his eyes made up Egyptian-style.

There's a sharp intake of breath as Madison is struck by a jolting epiphany. How could she have been so blind? Sterling didn't steal Eddie. Eddie had never been hers to begin with, at least not in the way she thought he was. Eddie Breyer is gay!

A rush of emotion surges through her,

sweeping away a clutter of mispercep-tions. After a dizzying moment of reorientation, she marshals her courage and walks up to the boys. Eddie and Jimi eye her warily.

'You're not going to scratch our eyes out, are you?' says Eddie, from beneath his long forelock.

'I'm sorry Eddie,' she says. 'I really am. I'm sorry I was so horrid. I was mistaken about a lot of things. I wish I could take it all back.'

Eddie studies her face for signs of aggression or insincerity, but all he sees is a contrite girl with big brown eyes and freckles across her nose.

'Yes, you were *terribly* horrid,' he says. 'Wasn't she Jimi?'

'Yes, the most terribly horrid person I've ever known.'

Then Eddie smiles and she smiles back. He reaches out and pulls her into a solid embrace. 'I should have been honest with you,' he said, 'but I couldn't even be honest with myself back then. Forgive me?' She nods her head.

Coach looks dismissively at the three of

them and walks to the front of the room for one last look at Sterling Seabright. He stands stiffly at the casket, looking down with no more emotion than if he were picking out a head of lettuce at IGA. After a few seconds, he walks away, speaks briefly to the Seabrights and stands at the far back corner of the room.

'Someone worked your dad over,' says Jimi.

'I noticed,' says Eddie. 'He looks like he's off his game today.'

Madison remains diplomatically silent. 'Excuse me guys,' she says. 'I have to do something.' She looks up at Eddie. 'Friends?'

'Friends,' he says.

Madison removes something from her hobo bag. She walks to the casket . . . a white casket with pink enamel roses on the sides and solid brass handles. She looks at Sterling one last time and wonders if her friend would have returned on Sunday if she could have. Maybe they could have patched things up. When she walks back up the aisle, a small perfume bottle is tucked beneath the edge of Sterling's satin pillow.

Madison forgot to sign the funeral book and returns to the vestibule. There's a long list of names above her signature: Robely Danner, Frank Tilsley, Carl Hammond, Mickey Lunn, Neville Gregory, Eldron Breyer, Jimi Whitleaf . . .

Wait a minute. Eldron Breyer?

She'd heard Coach called El by fellow teachers, but she heard it as L, like the initial of a first name, Leonard or Larry or something. Her mind flashes back to the diary. *E.B.*. What if Sterling had been involved, not with Eddie, but with Eldron? If that were true, Sterling's puzzling remark on the night of the fight made sense. '*He wasn't supposed to be home tonight*.' Sterling hadn't gone to see Eddie. She was there to see Eldron, the man who'd promised to get her on the boys' basketball team. Finally, things were making sense.

Eddie and Jimi decide to go for coffee before the mourners migrate to the church. Madison catches them at the door.

'Eddie, had you planned to be home

the night I caught up with Sterling?'

'The night of the fight? No. I'd planned to see a movie but it was no longer playing, so I invited Carl over instead.'

'Thank you, that's all I needed to know.'

'Why, what's up?'

'Plenty. I'll tell you later in private.'

⋆ ⋆ ⋆

Breyer stays only as long as convention demands.

'Coach Breyer?' He'd almost made it through the vestibule to the double glass doors when he turns to the girl with the strawberry-blonde hair and the hobo bag over her shoulder. She looks like an urchin in ugly shoes and a wilted cotton dress. The testimonials had begun and there was no one else in the vestibule.

'Yes?' he says, impatient to leave this whole mess behind him.

'I'm Madison Buckley.'

'Of course. Eddie's friend.'

'I was Sterling's friend too. Were you able to make headway with Mr. Gregory?'

'Whatever do you mean?'

'Getting Sterling on the boys' team.'

Breyer raises his arms and lets them fall defenselessly at his side.

'That rumor is pure fabrication.'

'Really?'

'I only knew her by reputation.'

'What if I told you that your association with Sterling is memorialized in print, Coach Breyer?'

His eyes vapor-lock on her face. There's an intelligence in her eyes that puts him on edge and he has the unsettling feeling this is one book he can't judge by its cover. Finally, he says, 'Memorialized in print? I don't know what that means.'

'She entrusted me with her diary.'

'Her what?' He swallows, then swallows again, like a fish bone is lodged in his throat.

'Her diary. I was asked to hold it in case something happened to her. I didn't think much about it at the time, except something has happened and now I *am* thinking about it.' He doesn't say anything, but a vein pulses in his neck.

'What is it, Coach? Are you alright?'

'Yes, of course I'm alright. Do you have it with you? The diary I mean.'

'I'm not through reading it,' she says, evasively. 'I owe her that much, don't you think?' His eyes shift from her face to the hobo bag. It's made of fringed brown suede with a strong zipper, big enough to carry a small dog and half a dozen books.

'That's all well and good,' he says, 'but you understand, her passing changes everything.'

'In what way?'

'You're too young to grasp the legalities, but it belongs to her parents now.' He takes a step toward her and extends his hand. 'I'll make sure they get it at the appropriate time.'

'I don't need a middleman. They're right in the next room. Don't you think that if she wanted her parents to have it, she'd have given it to them? There could be things she doesn't want them to know, things like sneaking off to cabins and motel rooms.'

Except for red finger-size welts on his face, he's turned ghost white. She's certain now. It's him. Eldron Breyer killed Sterling Seabright. The knowledge emboldens her.

'I don't doubt that it's full of juvenile ranting and fantasies,' he says, with a tight smile.

'I'm not sure I agree. A diary is a place where a girl can be honest about what's going on in her life, write down things she can't confide to anyone else. I've been thinking that a document by the victim of an unsolved murder is worth something.'

'A document? I'm not following you.'

'A testament in her own hand. If I can sell it to one of those unsolved crime shows on TV, I could save my parents' farm. I wouldn't have to go to the Christmas dance in a Goodwill gown.'

'That may be true, Madison, but I'd hate to see a nice girl like you lose your moral compass for a little money.'

She pauses before responding, her gaze cool and unblinking.

'For a *little* money, I wouldn't,' she says.

He studies her demeanor. Is she a naïve child with a greedy streak, or a conniving little wench trying to shake him down? How much does she suspect? How much does she know? And the biggest question of all. What's in the diary?

'Let me buy you lunch, Madison. We'll find a nice quiet place where we can talk, then I'll drop you off at the church.'

She's so hungry, the thought of food almost makes her faint.

'Coach Breyer?'

'Yes, Madison?'

'I'm never going to be that hungry . . . or that foolish.'

21

I kick off my shoes and collapse on the bed in my lacy underthings. The day's been emotionally exhausting and although it's late and the sun is low in the sky, I still have to pick up Frack so we can meet with Harry Fiegel at the jail.

Fargo jumps on the bed and flops down beside me. He's big and fluffy and warm. If I lie here another second, I'll fall asleep. He looks at me adoringly. I kiss his nose and ruffle his ears. If you want to be loved unconditionally, a dog's the ticket. They might eat you out of house and home and hog the bed, but they won't break your heart or steal your credit cards. I give him a big hug and pull myself up while I still have the energy. In twenty minutes I'm showered and back in uniform. Halfway out the door and the phone rings. I pause and let the machine pick up.

'Robely, it's Tammy. I wanted to . . . oh

shoot! A customer . . . Catch you later.'

I guess I'm not the only one having a busy day.

* * *

'All of the blonde hairs on Barnes' clothes belong to Karen Patterson,' says Harry, when we meet at the jail. 'Not one is from the Seabright girl.'

'How can you be so sure?' asks Frack. 'It's too soon for DNA results.'

'We don't need DNA. The ones taken from Bucky's clothes are microscopically dissimilar. Miss Seabright was a natural blonde. Karen Patterson is also blonde, but her hair has been chemically treated to achieve a lighter shade. They all belong to Miss Patterson.'

'But, that doesn't necessarily rule him out as the killer of Sterling Seabright. He was probably wearing something else the night she was murdered,' I say.

'You don't have to be a bloodhound to know this guy hasn't changed clothes since Neanderthals lived in caves. Officer Duhamel says they're the same duds he saw the night Bucky was pushing the bike: same oil stains, road dirt and McDonald's secret sauce.'

'We'd still like a word with him,' says Frack.

'Okay, knock yourself out. By the way, here's the cuffs he came in with.'

We clip the cuffs to our belts as we walk down the hall. When we enter the interrogation room with its scarred walls and stark furnishings, we see a steel chair bolted to the floor and Bucky's hands cuffed and chained to a metal ring between his legs. Even restrained, he looks like he could pump up his bulk and rip the chair from its mooring. We sit across from him with a narrow table between us. Despite his size and strength his expression is one of a contrite, slightly confused child.

'Geez lady, what happened to your face?' he says.

If I look at Frack I'm going to laugh. 'It's too hard to explain,' I tell him. 'You would have to have been there. Deputy Tilsley and I have a few questions for you regarding the night Officer Duhamel helped you with your bike.'

'I don't want to talk about last night.'

'This is in regard to a girl who died in the woods the night your bike quit on you.'

'What girl? I never took any girl into the woods.'

'We're hoping you might remember something that could help us with our investigation.'

'Okay, but I don't go into the woods. I get poison ivy. I was pushing my bike is all.' It's obvious the guy is developmentally disabled, otherwise he wouldn't have a swastika on his forehead and barbwire tattoos around his neck.

'When you were pushing your bike,' Frack continues, 'did you notice anything suspicious, someone going in or coming out of the woods, a man or a young woman with long blonde hair?'

'I'd remember that. I love girls with long blonde hair, but they always get me in trouble.'

'Yes, I know. How about a car on the shoulder of the road or . . . '

'There was a car, an older brown

Chevy. It come up behind me going south toward Ogdensburg. After it passed by, it started zigzagging across the line and almost hit a pickup coming in the opposite direction. That I remember. Reminds me of the time me and my old lady was fightin' in the car and she grabbed the wheel.'

'And you're sure about the car? Brown Chevy sedan.'

'That's right. I know my cars.'

'Did you see who was in it? A man, a woman, one person or two?'

'No. It was too dark.'

'Did you see the car again?'

'After I pushed the bike for another fifteen minutes or so, the Chevy was sitting at the edge of the ditch with the passenger door open, but nobody was in it.'

'Did you hear anything, a commotion, a lady screaming, a man yelling?'

'No, nuthin' like that. Just the wind in the trees, maybe an owl or two. When the officer showed up I looked back and the car was gone.'

'Did it pass you or turn around and go

back the way it came?'

'I don't know. I wasn't paying attention. Can I go home now? I wanna get bailed out.'

'That's not our decision,' I say.

'But, my little boy is getting baptized on Sunday morning. My girlfriend is going to be pissed off if I'm not there.'

'I'm afraid you're going to miss that, Buckster,' says Frack, 'but if they let you out on good behavior, you might make his college graduation.'

* * *

I can tell that Frack's hand is bothering him, so I take the wheel on the way back to Abundance. It's dark, with a frigid wind rustling the trees. We look into the darkness when we pass the section of woods where the homicide occurred. It's a place we're not likely to forget, no matter how many times we drive these roads.

'We finally have a description of the car,' I say. 'Everything Bucky told us confirms our theory of how this happened.'

'More accurately stated, it doesn't contradict it.'

'True. I agree with Harry though. Barnes is dangerous, but he isn't good for the Seabright murder. If he were, she wouldn't have been found fully clothed. Besides, Sterling could have outrun a deer and Barnes is as slow and dull as mud.'

'You may be right, but I'm still not ready to give him a free pass.'

'What about the brown car?' I ask. 'His story explains the tracks we saw above the ditch. It's either owned by someone who can't afford a better one or it's the killer's winter car. I think the driver of that car set out to kill Sterling that night and things exploded prematurely. She'd become your proverbial inconvenient woman. You know the ratio of homicides among pregnant women? It's off the charts. What if the killer had a wife and Sterling was threatening to tell? Even if he's single he wouldn't want to get stuck with child support payments for the next eighteen years.'

'Or get crucified for planking an

underage girl?' says Frack. 'We don't know the age of the person she was involved with. It might have been someone her age, or maybe someone older who couldn't afford a scandal.'

'Which brings us back to Wexler and Breyer and miscellaneous parties unknown,' I say.

'It does. So, what now?'

'I think we're so tired we're starting to go in circles. I'll drop you off so you can get some sleep and we'll go at it again in the morning. You brace Breyer and I'll take another shot at Madison and Carl. If that doesn't point us in a promising direction, we'll go back to The Alcola and have a go at Wexler again. I have that creepy-crawly feeling at the back of my neck that tells me things are about to bust wide open.'

'You want to get something to eat?' says Frack.

'I'm too exhausted to eat. If I sit down I won't be able to get back up. I'm going to the station to check the mail and return a call from Tammy. Then I'm going home.' We approach the Little Papoose

and I can't help looking toward the bar.
'You talk to her yet?'
'Gladys? No, she needs to pout a while. I did the right thing, at least for myself, but I still feel uneasy about it.'
'Don't. You can't fix other people, Robely. They have to fix themselves.'
We pass the Stop and Go. Tammy's shift is over and she's gone home. We cruise through town and pull in front of Frack's house. 'Here we are,' I say.
Frack's place is a solid two-story Victorian on half an acre lot overlooking the town square. It has buttercream paint with white trim, a monkey puzzle tree out front and a big garden area in the back. He puts his arm over my shoulder and leans into me. He has the comforting smell of smoke in his clothes and I feel the heat coming off his skin.
'Don't even think about it,' I say. 'We're under a streetlight and old Gracie Tindle next door is peeking through her curtains.'
'You are one hard woman.'
There's a clever retort on my tongue, but I decide not to go there.

22

Carl and Madison sit with Eddie and Jimi through the church Mass and hook up again at the graveside. There are no dry eyes when 'Amazing Grace' is squeezed through the bagpipes. As a final gesture the four friends drop white roses on the casket. They hug and say their goodbyes and Carl and Madison walk between the gravestones to the car. It's getting dark and the melancholy notes of the dying season float in the wind.

'I've never been so wiped out,' says Madison, looking at Carl. 'Once Father O'Bannion starts talking you can't shut him up. I'm never going to another funeral unless it's my own.'

'Don't say that. It's bad luck,' he says, opening her car door.

They buckle up and Madison tosses her hobo bag on the floor beneath the dash. Carl notices the goose-bumps on her arms and turns on the heater as soon as the engine warms up. He looks in the rear-view mirror and sees a car pull out the moment he pulls away from the curb. It creeps along at a distance as he drives toward the cemetery exit. He has the feeling that he's being watched. When he turns into the street the car lets him get a head start, then follows.

'I could swear that car was parked down from my house a couple nights ago,' he says. 'Look back and tell me what you see.'

Madison shifts around in her seat and rolls the window down. 'It's a pretty generic-looking vehicle.'

'Can you see who's behind the wheel?'

'It's too far away.' She rolls the window back up. By the time they turn onto the highway the car is gone.

'I'm absolutely starved,' says Carl. He looks over at Madison in her sad little dress and worn shoes. She's a tiger in a small package. She can be opinionated and disagreeable, but he respects how she keeps her grades up despite the problems at home. 'When is the last time you ate?'

'Breakfast. Peanut butter.'

'How does the Blue Bird Café sound? I'm buying.'

'It sounds like a Roman Bacchanal without the sex and wine.'

'You're clever. You have a unique way of expressing yourself.'

'That's what Sterling said, *clever and fun to be with*. Sometimes I'm too clever for my own good.'

'Why do you say that?' The moon rides low on the horizon and disappears as the woods encroach from both sides of the road. She gives him a look, solemn and unreadable.

'What?' he says, studying her face. She's wound tight, like a fiddle string that's about to snap. He switches to high beams as they hit a straight stretch of road. Twice he slows the car to avoid deer. 'Is there something you want to tell me?'

'I have Sterling's diary.'

'What?

'It's true. I took it from her house on Saturday. I didn't know she was dead.'

'Why?'

'Why do you think? She treated us

poorly and I was angry. I wanted to know her secrets.'

'And do you?'

Madison's stomach clenches painfully around the grinding emptiness in her stomach. She feels dizzy and faint and leans forward, hugging her mid-section.

'Never mind,' he says. 'You can tell me over a double cheeseburger.'

She looks over at him, her cheek resting on her knees, her penny-bright hair tumbling over her face. 'I wasn't sure until today, but I know who killed Sterling Seabright.'

* * *

Before I lock up the station for the night I call Tammy.

'My machine picked up your call,' I say. 'How's Mike?'

'He's slightly better, but I need to talk to you about something else.'

'Are the triplets okay?'

'Oh, yes. You can tell they're a cop's kids. Their shrieks sound like police whistles.'

I laugh out load. 'Thanks for the heads up. I think I'll delay intimate encounters until my childbearing years are behind me.'

'If you've got five minutes I've got something juicy for you,' she says. 'You got my wheels turning when we were talking about Coach. I knew there'd been some scuttlebutt a while back, but I wasn't all that curious at the time.'

'How about now?'

'Oh, you bet. I made a call to a teacher friend, Dodie Elfman, who's retired from the Green Bay School District. Once she started talking about Eldron Breyer, I couldn't shut her up, nor did I try.'

'You've got my attention,' I say.

'Dodie says that Coach Breyer left Green Bay under a cloud of suspicion.'

'Suspicion of what?'

'He was teaching gym and math at the time. An incorrigible fourteen-year-old girl had been transferred there after several arrests for shoplifting and sexual promiscuity. She'd been going to school on the bad side of town and her probation officer thought that a transfer to a better environment might straighten her out. She had Breyer for bonehead math.'

'She sounds like a tough cookie.'

'You're probably envisioning some tattooed chick with thundering biceps and no neck, but Dodie said that Kindy Sinclair was a little silver butterfly. Those were her very words. Little silver butterfly. She was four foot eleven, eighty-five pounds with silver-blonde hair and eyes the color of a robin's egg. That doesn't mean she wasn't hell on wheels, but she was no lady wrestler either.'

I hear the triplets raising hell in the background. Tammy takes a long drag on a cigarette, coughs out the smoke and takes a drink from something rattling with ice cubes.

'Tommy! Trevor! Travis! You kids stop running in the house,' she yells.

'Tammy, don't stop now.'

'Okay, so this anonymous caller gets on the phone to the cops and says Coach and the girl were seen making out in a car at lunchtime.'

'What? Where?'

'By the Fox River behind the school.'

'That's quite a story. Was it a crank call or was there something to it?'

'For obvious reasons, they both denied it, but I say where there's smoke there's fire. The thing is, the cops had nothing solid to go on.' I hear the ice cubes again.

'Except?' My pulse ratchets up a notch or two.

'Another teacher who had her suspicions rifled through Breyer's car and found Kindy's cute little panties in his glove compartment.'

'No kidding! That's pretty damning.'

'When she finally confessed to going all the way with Breyer, the school was afraid of law suits and all the adults closed ranks. Her probation officer said she was capable of cunning subterfuge. Who are people going to believe, a kid with a record of misconduct or a solid citizen who's never had so much as a speeding ticket?'

'Implying she planted the panties herself?' I say.

'That's what it sounds like.'

'That doesn't make any sense at all.'

'She was moved to yet another school and the dust finally settled. This was toward the end of the school year and by the time class started last September, Coach had landed in Abundance. Whether he left voluntarily or under pressure is anyone's guess, but I'm sure they were glad to see him go.'

'Didn't Gregory do a background check?'

'It wouldn't have mattered. There was no paper trail since charges were never filed. The entire matter was swept under the rug.'

'I'm going to look into this, Tammy. It's a lot to swallow in one gulp.'

'Well swallow this,' she says, with a tipsy laugh. 'Giving up her party favors should at least have earned her an A. Instead, he had the gall to flunk her. How unfair is that?'

'I wonder if her parents would allow me to talk with her. It's important. There's a chance it ties in with the case Frack and I are working on.'

'I need to backtrack here. Talking with them wouldn't make any difference.'

'What do you mean?'

'I should have mentioned this in the beginning. Kindy hanged herself the summer after the scandal broke.'

'My god!' I gasp. 'That's horrible.'

'Gotta go, Robely. The kids are beating each other with Tonka trucks. Don't forget, we get our delivery of cheese curds in the morning. I'll save you a bag.'

23

Carl and Madison park behind the café. They slip inside a split second before Molly reaches the door with the key. The radio is turned to golden oldies. 'Blueberry Hill' gives way to 'Rock Around the Clock' as they take an orange Naugahyde booth in the far corner.

Madison wilts onto the seat and plops the hobo bag down beside her. Her flimsy summer dress is no protection from the cold and Carl has wrapped his sports coat around her shoulders. A final customer gets out of his car and races for the door, but Molly turns the key and flips the sign to closed.

'Don't bother with the menu,' she says, approaching their booth. Her face is flushed and most of the pins have fallen out of her bun. 'You have a choice of cheeseburgers and fries or cheeseburgers and fries and I'll give you fifteen minutes to wolf them down. My feet are killing me and I want to go home.'

'Geez Molly, you don't have to be so snappy,' says Carl.

'Yes, I do. If you stay one minute longer you'll have to massage my bunions.'

Madison can't contain her giggles.

'Go ahead and laugh,' says Molly. 'Wait until you get to be my age.'

'You're only forty,' says Madison.

'That's 240 in dog years and I feel every day of it.'

'Let's get to it then,' says Carl. 'While we're waiting for the burgers we'll have apple pie a la mode and chocolate shakes.'

'Your wish is my command, master.'

After their pie arrives, Carl leans across the table toward Madison. 'I think you'd better tell me what's going on,' he says. 'Then I'll tell you what I've been holding back. There's only one thing we can do for Sterling now and that's help Danner and Tilsley nail the person who killed her.'

'Are you still in love with her?'

The question takes him by surprise. He hears an expectant note in her voice.

'No, Madison, I'm not. I was in love with the person I wanted her to be, but that person never existed.'

'That's sort of the way I feel about Eddie,' she says, 'but, Eddie's a good person and I still want to be his friend.'

'You will be. We'll all be friends.'

Madison slides the diary across the table. 'I've marked the relevant passages, but I still don't know *why* she was murdered.'

'Shh! I'm reading. I already know why.'

By the time he closes the diary, she's finished her pie. 'E.B. is Eldron Breyer,' he says. 'That's a no-brainer.'

'I was so convinced it was Eddie that it took me a long time to figure that out. I mean, who would guess Sterling was carrying on with Coach? He's good-looking and everything, but he strikes me as being . . . I don't know . . . vain and self-absorbed.'

'So was she.'

'I guess you're right.' Molly returns with the cheeseburgers and picks up the twenty beside Carl's plate.

'Keep the change,' he says.

'There is no change, smart ass.'

'It wasn't until I told him about the diary at the visitation that I knew for sure it was him,' says Madison. 'You should have seen how desperate he was to get his hands on it. Now I've got a tiger by the tail and I don't know how to let go. Even if he was getting it on with Sterling, it doesn't seem motive enough for murder. These things between teachers and students have always gone on. In fact, my great grandmother married her teacher. He was fifteen years her senior. She was sixteen and nobody thought anything of it.'

'Times have changed, Madison. Besides, your great-grandfather had honorable intentions and I doubt that your grandmother was pregnant.'

'What?'

'That's right. As far as I know, I'm the only one she told, with the possible exception of the person who killed her. She said either I was responsible or one other guy, but she wouldn't say who. I can *prove* it wasn't me, so it has to be Breyer.'

'She should have been honest with us,'

says Madison. 'Maybe, she'd still be alive.'

'You should have told me about the diary.'

'You should have told me she was pregnant.'

They point fingers at one another until they can't keep a straight face.

'I guess there's enough *should haves* to go around,' he says.

'Shoulda, woulda, coulda. Sterling was always so sensible before she met him. Selfish, but focused. I don't understand how he took her in. It was obviously an unworkable alliance from the beginning.'

'He's a charmer. He has that bouncy boyish quality that makes him approachable, like he's your big brother or your best friend.'

'He's probably done this kind of thing before,' says Madison.

'He knew how much Sterling loved honors and first-place ribbons and publicity, so he promised to get her on the boys' basketball team.'

'Even though he knew it would never happen.'

'That's right,' he says. 'He kept dangling the carrot, leading her on.' Wind howls around the corner of the building and leaves blow against the window. The lights flicker ominously and power lines beyond the window whip in the wind. 'I think we're in for a wild night.' He closes the diary and Madison slips it in her bag. 'You realize we can't just sit on this information.'

'There was a light on in the sheriff's station,' says Madison. 'Someone's working late.'

'Are you ready to give up the diary?' he asks.

'Are you ready to tell everything you know?'

Carl pops the last French fry in his mouth. 'Come on, let's do it,' he says.

* * *

After talking with Tammy, I feel a sense of urgency. I hate disturbing Frack, but I don't feel comfortable putting this off until morning. I need to bring Eldron Breyer in for questioning and I don't want to do it alone. As I pick up the phone and punch in Frack's number I see a brown Chevy pass the station for the third time in twenty minutes. It's too dark to see who's behind the wheel. It drifts slowly to the corner and turns right toward the school. Frack answers on the third ring.

'I hope you haven't turned in yet.'

'No, just having a beer and unwinding to some slow blue jazz. Why, you want to come over?'

I tell him about the brown Chevy and my conversation with Tammy.

'You'd better come get me.'

* * *

Carl walks toward the car with his arm around Madison's shoulders, wind cutting through their clothes and whipping their hair.

'Can you feel the ice in the wind?' he says.

'What?'

'The wind . . . never mind.'

As Carl opens the passenger door and

Madison gets in, a figure steps from the darkness and something heavy and metallic comes down on Carl's skull. He drops to the asphalt without a sound, his head striking the sharp edge of the car door.

There's a violent tug on Madison's hobo bag. She lets out a cry and hunkers down on the car seat, hugging the bag close to her body. An arm reaches around her side and fumbles for the zipper. Madison sinks her teeth into the arm. Despite the jacket she gets a sizeable pinch of muscle and clamps down hard. When he jerks free and lets fly a litany of obscenities, she recognizes the voice of Coach Breyer.

His backhand catches her in the face and flips an internal switch. Her fear turns to fury. She has to take whatever Mavis dishes out, but she doesn't have to take it from anybody else. His voice grates in her ear. 'Let go of the bag!'

'No!'

'All I want is the diary, you obnoxious brat. I'll burn it and no one will be the wiser.'

But, it's not about the diary anymore. It isn't even about Sterling Seabright. It's about power and powerlessness, about knowing your currency and owning it. It's about the bank trying to steal the farm, being sent to school in raggedy clothes and missing out on the last of the jelly. The back door of the café opens and Molly steps beneath the dim glow of the exit light. Breyer drags Madison out of the car by her hair.

'Molly! Call 911!' she screams into the wind. '911!'

'What?'

A sleek black handgun appears in Breyer's hand. Fire spits from the muzzle next to Madison's ear and a bullet hits the door inches above Molly's head. She ducks back inside and a bolt scrapes in place. Breyer yells something, but the concussion from the gun has deafened her in one ear.

'Let go of my hair,' she cries. 'Are you crazy?'

Carl moans and struggles to his knees. He grabs Breyer's pants leg, but suffers a kick to the ribs and another to the side of the head. He feels the warmth of blood on his face and tickling down the back of his shirt.

Breyer shoves Madison into the front seat of the Chevy, slams the door and hops behind the wheel. She reaches for the door handle, but it's been removed . . . everything premeditated . . . everything planned in advance.

As the car bounces out of the lot, it hits a speed bump, sparks flying from beneath the chassis. Molly stands inside the front window with the phone to her ear, reciting Breyer's license plate number to the 911 operator. Despite the wound to his head and his vision blurred, Carl stumbles to his car and takes off after the Chevy.

24

As soon as I pull up to the Victorian, Frack trots down the steps to the car. The windstorm has littered the street with fallen branches, dead leaves and acorns. He's about to get into the passenger side of the patrol car when the brown Chevy I'd seen just minutes ago flies by. As it passes beneath the halo of the streetlight I get a glimpse of Madison Buckley and a man with curly auburn hair. Breyer! Half a block behind the Chevy, Carl Hammond, his face bloodied, is in pursuit.

'Breyer has Madison Buckley!' I yell.

'I'll drive,' he says.

I slide over, unsnapping my holster and clamping the seatbelt in place. Frack guns the car, pressing me against the back of the seat as we launch. The patrol car has a strong engine and Frack is an excellent driver at high speeds, so I'm not anticipating a dramatic or prolonged made-for-the-movies car chase. He steers with his left hand and bandaged right forearm. The siren screams and the light bar flashes as we enter the chase. On the outskirts of town, Breyer swings onto Highway 22 in the direction of Symco, an unincorporated blip on the map, popular for its annual tractor pull.

The road is empty, the lights on in farmhouse bedrooms, everyone shuttered in for the night. We sweep around a deep curve, pass an abandoned house and a collapsing barn on our right. It's a stretch of rolling fields, stands of desiccated corn and dark windbreaks. Frack floors it and passes Carl's car as if it were standing still. Inch by inch we close on the Chevy. Up ahead I see shifting shadows at the roadside and a family of three deer materializes from the darkness.

'Deer!' I yell.

A large buck and two young does burst into the headlights of the Chevy. The buck leaps the car and makes it safely across the road. Breyer slams on his brakes and twists the steering wheel sharply to the left. A large doe hits the side of his car with the force of a wrecking ball. The younger doe catapults into the air and lands on the hood, its body shattering the windshield. Breyer's car upends on two left wheels and I hear myself yelling, 'No, no, no!' It wobbles for thirty feet when a tire blows, sending it catapulting into the ditch with a terrific thud.

'Judas Priest! This is a disaster,' I yell, as Frack pulls over and I radio for assistance. Carl pulls in behind us and the three of us run to the overturned vehicle.

Frack and I scramble up the side. The passenger side door is now on the top of the car, a deep concave crease wedging it tightly into the frame.

'I've got it,' I say, thinking of Frack's injured hand, but he attacks it without hesitation, throwing every muscle, bone and tendon into the effort. Blood from his ripped stitches soaks through his bandage and drips onto the surface of the car. The door finally screeches and scrapes open a few inches and I get my hands in the opening. Together we pull it up halfway where it stops and refuses to open wider. Madison hangs downward from her seatbelt like a rag doll, but I see no sign of Eldron Breyer.

'I'll hold the door,' says Frack. 'See if you can unhook her seatbelt.'

Carl climbs up next to me. I smell gasoline and hear it dripping under the car from the ruptured fuel tank.

'Carl, I want you on the other side of the road before this thing blows. Now!'

'It's going to take two of us to get her out,' he says. I know he's right.

There's no time to argue or wait for first responders to determine Madison's condition before she's moved. If we don't act immediately, we're all going to be blown to kingdom come. Carl gets his hands under her arms and lifts her up so I can unlatch her seatbelt. We untangle her and each taking an arm, lift her free of the car. She's dazed but conscious and Carl carries her to the opposite side of the road. Frack lets the door slump back down, seemingly unaware that his bandage is soaked through with blood.

We jump in the ditch in search of Breyer. I see an arm sticking out from under the car. I drop to my knees and feel for a pulse, then shake my head. He's beyond help, crushed under the weight of the vehicle. We turn our attention to the deer.

The doe that broadsided the car lies dead in the road from a broken neck. The smaller doe has slipped off the hood and stands in the ditch on trembling legs, stunned and disoriented. Moving closer we see a four-inch laceration on her haunch and a few superficial cuts from the safety glass.

'Look,' says Frack, pointing toward the field. The buck is standing perfectly still twenty feet away. He's a magnificent thick-coated animal with a great rack of antlers crowning his head. As we watch him, the wind down-shifts and dies. A deep silence falls over the fields and the first silver snowflakes of the season swirl through the moonlight and settle on the buck's mahogany coat.

'He's waiting for her,' says Frack. 'He afraid of us, but he's not leaving without her.'

As I watch the buck stand his ground, an emotion I can't define sweeps over me and the goose-bumps rise on my arms. We slowly approach the doe and gently turn her until she's facing the field. The buck shakes his antlers and paws the ground. Her ears prick and her eyes focus. Frack gives her a tap on the rump. 'Go,' he says. 'Go home.' She walks shakily up the side of the ditch to where the buck is waiting. They touch noses. He rubs his neck against her side, then they turn toward the windbreak and melt like spirits into the trees.

'I hope they make it, Frack. I hope they make it to the end of hunting season.'

'Me too,' he says.

I hear ominous popping noises.

'Run!' I shout.

We barely make it across the road when there's a whoosh and the Chevy goes off like a bomb. The four of us crouch and cover our heads as the concussion from the blast whips through our hair and clothes. Frack positions himself between me and the flaming debris raining down from the sky and Carl covers Madison's head with his coat. It's a full minute before it's safe enough to stand.

I remove my muffler and wrap it around Carl's neck to stem the bleeding. His eyes are clear and alert, no sign that he's gone into shock.

'How's Madison doing?' asks Frack.

'She's shaken up, but nothing's broken,' says Carl. 'If it weren't for the seatbelt they'd both be under that car.'

I hear sirens in the distance and look at the teenagers huddled together at my side.

'The first responders are going to check you two out,' I tell them. 'If the doctors at the E.R. clear you and you're not at the station by noon tomorrow, you're getting a house call complete with sirens and flashing lights. It'll give your neighbors something to talk about for a year. You got that?'

'We'll be there,' says Carl. 'I never lied to you.'

'Telling part of the truth is the same as lying,' says Frack. 'You both held out on us and your silence could have gotten us all killed.'

'We saw your light on at the station tonight,' says Madison. 'We were on our way to give you the diary and tell you everything we knew when Breyer attacked us.'

'Are we talking about the diary you took from Sterling's room?'

'Yes,' she says, finally giving in to the truth. The flames continue to roar and spiral into the sky. 'There goes my hobo bag,' says Madison. 'There goes the diary. Breyer said he was going to burn it, but I don't think this is what he had in mind.'

Carl pulls the coat more snugly around her shoulders as the snowflakes whip around their heads. 'We don't need it anymore,' he says. 'The bad guy just got the death penalty.'

We stand at the edge of the road stomping our feet and blowing white clouds of breath into the night air. We watch the fire rage and snow collect in the dark branches of the trees. It's the decisive moment when autumn turns and walks away without a backward glance and we're thrown into the deep freeze until June of next year.

We're startled when a lesser explosion sends a smoking object clattering to my feet. Curious, I pick it up with my handkerchief and know immediately what I'm looking at. It's a black glass cell phone in a melting pink case. I show it to Frack. 'This is Sterling Seabright's missing phone.'

'When she jumped out of Breyer's car that night, it must have slid under the seat,' he says. 'Look, the ringer's been off all this time. If he knew it was there he would have gotten rid of it. This is one hell of a piece of incriminating evidence. If we're lucky it's retained vital information.'

'Look,' says Madison, as the fire truck roars toward our position with its array of whistles and bells and flashing lights. 'The circus has come to town.'

25

It is six weeks later. Frack and I lie in bed on a snowy Saturday morning in his big house overlooking the town square. Fargo is licking his paws in front of the crackling fireplace, his shiny tags jingling from a new red collar. Both Mike and Sheriff Ernie Brooker are back on the job and Sherry's been at her desk long enough to lose her Florida tan. The Blonde Beauty Case is closed and the last time I drove down Cloverdale Cut there was a 'for sale' sign in front of the Seabright farm.

'There was enough data in that phone to put our case to rest to everyone's satisfaction,' says Frack. 'I swear it fell from the sky like manna from heaven.'

'That and finding the gun under the car that was used to shoot poor Betsy Warren. We could have wrapped it up sooner if Carl and Madison had been more forthcoming,' I say.

'They were protecting secrets of their

own and they weren't sure if they'd get a fair shake. We are, after all, the dreaded fuzz,' says Frack, giving me a little tickle.

'Oh, Frack!' I laugh. 'That expression went out with love beads and bell bottoms.'

'I saw Madison and Carl in the Blue Bird yesterday. I think they've become an item.'

'That's nice. They have good futures ahead of them,' I say. 'Sterling's misadventure will keep them from making any foolish mistakes. Madison wants to go into law. You watch. That girl is going to kick butt. When I saw her last, her cheeks had filled out. She was wearing a new red coat and fur-trimmed ski boots.'

'Those clothes didn't come from selling goat cheese.'

'I'm sure you're right.'

'You know what I'm implying.'

'I do and I for one don't care if they robbed the community bank with a Tommy gun. The Buckleys deserve a little good luck.'

'Some cop you are,' he says, playfully mussing my hair. 'Well, we finally have a day off at the same time. What do you want to do with it?'

'Stay in bed until noon for starters.'

'Me too.'

'Mrs. Stebbins gave us tickets for tonight's performance of *Hamlet* with Eddie in the title role. He's gained liberated minor status from the courts when he proved he could support himself as the sole heir of the Coronetti family fortune.'

'Did she say if he still plans to go to San Francisco?'

'He's trading San Francisco for Paris, would you believe. He and Jimi are leaving right after graduation.'

'Wow!'

'Let's go tonight,' I say. 'He'd be thrilled if we came.'

'You mean so we can watch him die as no one else can?'

'For heaven's sake Frack, I'm sure there's a little more to it than that.'

I turn back to the morning paper and run my finger down the Lost and Found column.

'I can't believe it. Look at this,' I say.

‘*Small silver-plated jack-knife with engraved initials E.E. lost between Abundance and Weyauwega. Sentimental value. Call Earl Edwards, New London.*’

‘Earl Edwards? Let me see that,’ he says, snatching the paper away. I see the jagged white scars covering his hand and lower arm, all to save a deer everyone else wanted to put on the dinner table. Frack was right. He is my kind of guy. ‘You mean we spent all that time chasing initials that had no relevance to our case?’

‘I guess so. We were never certain from the beginning.’ We toss the paper aside, and propped back against our pillows, finish our morning coffee and watch the snow feather down on the town square.

‘I’m surprised old lady Tindle hasn’t made a fuss about your overnight visits,’ he says. ‘I thought she’d be banging at my door reciting some ancient moral’s clause.’

‘She’s not going to bother us. She likes me. I bought her off.’

‘You what?’

‘I bought her off.’

‘How did you manage that?’

'She's just a lonely old woman, Frack. I cheered her up with a bag of cheese curds and a fifth of brandy.'

'You are one conniving woman.' He rolls toward me and buries his face in my hair. 'Mmm,' he says, 'coconut shampoo.'

'From the Dollar Store.'

'What I want to know is how you're going to buy *me* off?'

'Let me show you,' I say. Our lips are an inch apart when an earthquake rocks the room and a big fluffy lump settles between us.

'Fargo! Off the bed!'

THE END

Other titles in the
Linford Mystery Library:

CONCERTO FOR FEAR

Norman Firth

1940s private detective Red Benton puts his ingenuity and charm to work in two stories of mystery and murder. *Concerto For Fear* features a murderous piano and a seemingly cursed new piece of music with a deadly low G. And in *Death Flows Down River*, two corpses are fished out of the water with curious neat incisions in their abdomens — and Red makes what turns out to be perhaps the worst mistake of his career when he sends an innocent woman on what he thinks is a routine investigation . . .

BREAKING THE RULES

Geraldine Ryan

Who broke into teacher Julia's car to steal Year Eleven's English coursework — and why? Attempting to solve the mystery, Julia soon finds herself *Breaking the Rules* . . . In *Running*, Mick Ashworth witnesses a murder. When he gives evidence in court, his family is put in jeopardy and they are forced to go into hiding under the witness protection scheme. Can they keep their new identities secret? And in *Beloved*, Helen begins a happy relationship with Stefan — but things soon start to take a sinister turn . . .

THE LITTLE GREY MAN

Norman Firth

Identical twins Jerry and Harold Mills are polar opposites. Jerry, hardworking and reliable, has made a success of his life and is engaged to the beautiful Andrea. But his brother soon exhibits his criminal nature and is forced to flee the country and disappear. Five years later, now a murderer and fugitive hiding in Marseilles, Harold writes to his brother, begging him for help. But when the brothers meet, Harold murders Jerry and assumes his identity, faking his own suicide. Then he returns to England, and Andrea . . .

DREAMS, DEMONS AND DEATH

John Burke

Psychic investigators are asked to help a man plagued by terrifying dreams that threaten his life . . . A young girl falls into a coma and dreams of another world — and when she wakes, she is no longer human . . . A family of musicians find themselves trapped in a remote village, forced to play the Devil's tune . . . A family celebration ends in a tragic death . . . During a row, a man kills his wife, but finds himself trapped in an even worse relationship . . . Seven stories of dreams, demons and death!